# Protecting the Future

# Protecting the Future

**SEAL of Protection**

**Book 8**

By Susan Stoker

This book is a work of fiction. Names, characters, places, and incidents are products of the author's imagination or are fictitiously. Any resemblance to actual events or locales or persons living or dead is entirely coincidental.



Cover Design by Chris Mackey, AURA Design Group

Manufactured in the United States

# Table of Contents

# Guide to the SEALs

Matthew "Wolf" Steel – Caroline Martin Steel

Christopher "Abe" Powers – Alabama Ford Smith Powers
Adopted Daughters: Brinique & Davisa

Hunter "Cookie" Knox – Fiona Storme Knox

Sam "Mozart" Reed – Summer James Pack Reed
Daughter: April

Faulkner "Dude" Cooper – Cheyenne Nicole Cotton Cooper
Unborn Daughter: As yet unnamed

Kason "Benny" Sawyer – Jessyka Allen Sawyer
Daughter: Sara
Son: John

John "Tex" Keegan – Melody Grace Keegan
Adopted Iraqi Daughter: Akilah

Patrick Hurt – Julie Lytle

# Prologue

*Our top story tonight is the kidnapping of four service members by the terrorist group ISIS in Syria. A new video has surfaced showing who is believed to be Sergeant Penelope Turner, once again declaring her allegiance to Allah and warning the United States and Great Britain that if they don't pull all troops out of the Middle East, the wrath of Allah will be brought down upon all Americans and Brits.*

*Sergeant Turner, along with three other Army personnel, was kidnapped about a month ago while she was on a humanitarian mission in Turkey. The refugee camps on the Syrian border have swelled to hundreds of thousands of people trying to escape the unrest in Syria. There's no running water and not a lot of food. The conditions are primitive, at best. The Turkish forces are doing all they can to deal with the influx of people, but it's simply not enough. The President authorized American troops to go in and assist with the situation. Turner and the other soldiers were kidnapped while patrolling a particularly dangerous section of the camp. Unfortunately, the men who were taken along with Turner were found two days later; they'd been strung up on crosses and burned alive.*

*There had been no word of Turner's fate until two weeks ago when the first video surfaced. She was wearing a veil, and while not much of her could be seen, officials say she sounded good and looked like she hadn't been heavily tortured.*

*Her fate is still unknown, and as of now, the government has no idea where she's being held. They continue to reassure her family that they are doing all they can to find and rescue her. Stay tuned for an interview with Penelope's brother, Cade Turner, a firefighter from San Antonio, Texas.*

# Chapter One

CAROLINE LAY IN bed with one arm slung over her husband's chest and idly ran her fingers over his nipple. They were both content and sated after making love for the second time that night.

"Do you think they'll ever find her?"

"Who, darlin'?"

"Penelope. That woman who was kidnapped in the Middle East."

Matthew "Wolf" Steel shifted under his wife and kissed her forehead lightly. "Probably not." He felt Caroline sigh as she turned her head into his chest and nuzzled farther into him.

"I can't help but imagine myself in her place," Caroline said sadly.

"Ice, I can't—"

"No, I know. It's not the same thing really at all, but every time they've shown that video of her and how she's probably being forced to say all those horrible things, all I can think of is that her tone doesn't match the look in her eyes."

"What do you mean?" Wolf asked, genuinely curious.

"She sounds meek and serious, but I swear, Matthew, her eyes look pissed. As if she's just waiting for her chance to turn around and kill all those men who are keeping her captive. And I see it because I know just how she feels. When I was kidnapped and that jerk was filming me, I was saying one thing, but deep inside felt something way different. And I was doing everything I could to send a message to you, and whoever else might watch that video, through my eyes. I know, it was stupid to think you could actually read what I wanted to say in my eyes, but inside I was thinking about how much I loved you. I was trying to tell you where I was, and I was pleading for you to come and find me. I could be wrong, but it's obvious, at least to me, that Penelope Turner is trying to say many of the same things."

Wolf turned until Caroline was on her back and he loomed over her. He braced himself up on an elbow and brushed a strand of her dark hair behind her ear with his other hand. She grabbed his biceps and looked up at him with such love, he still had to pinch himself sometimes to make sure it was real.

Three years had passed since he'd made her his wife, and every day since then he thanked his lucky stars they'd found each other. She made him happier than he'd ever been in his life.

"Yeah, I saw it back then as I watched you on tape, and I see it in Sergeant Turner now."

Caroline bit her lip, then asked, "Do you think they're…hurting her?"

Wolf kept his voice low and tried to sound reassuring. "It's hard to say. They're certainly keeping her for a reason, probably because she's small, blonde, and a woman. They want to force the world to pay more attention to them and take them seriously."

"You mean the bombing of that wedding last month didn't do it?" Caroline's tone showed her irritation.

Wolf shook his head, amazed that he could fall in love with his wife more every time she opened her mouth. He loved that she didn't take things at face value, that she felt deeply and wasn't afraid to speak her mind. "Unfortunately, no. They need something bigger than that. And kidnapping a group of Americans isn't big, not like on the scale that 9/11 was, but if they keep the U.S. distracted—and putting a beautiful, petite woman on television and making her say anti-American and anti-British things is distracting—perhaps they can work their way up to another grand gesture."

"I love you, Matthew."

Wolf smiled down at Caroline, not surprised at her change in subject. "I love you too, Ice."

"I'm also very proud of you."

"Thank you, baby. You've done some pretty awesome things yourself in your research too."

"I wasn't done," Caroline pouted, gripping Matthew's arms tighter.

"Sorry," Wolf chuckled. "Go ahead."

"I'm proud of you, but if you ever get kidnapped by those assholes, I'm gonna have to gather the girls, and Tex, and knock some heads."

"I'm not gonna get kidnapped. I hate to say it, but those soldiers didn't follow proper protocol. I'm not sure what happened, but they obviously separated from their unit in that refugee camp and didn't have backup. I don't know if they were lured away from the rest of their unit, if they simply didn't think they were in danger, or even if they were ordered to patrol without proper procedure being followed, but you know the team and I are always very careful, Ice. We'd never willingly expose ourselves to danger."

"Okay, I'm just saying."

Wolf smiled, leaned over, and kissed Caroline. "What time is this thing tomorrow?"

Caroline smiled hugely and Wolf eased down next to her onto the mattress again, letting Caroline snuggle into his chest once more. He never got tired of her affectionate nature, and the way she would immediately throw a leg over his, and how she'd curl into his side the second he lay down.

"Well, it's supposed to start at two, but I'm sure the others will trickle in as they can get there. Jess is always late, but I can't blame her. It has to suck trying to get two babies out and ready and gather up all the stuff she needs to bring with her. I swear, I've never seen so much baby stuff as she and Kason have!"

Wolf chuckled. "Yeah, and where did she get all that baby stuff?" He felt Caroline smile.

"Okay, me and the girls might have gone overboard two years ago, but Sara was the first baby born to any of us and we wanted to make sure Jess and Kason had everything they needed. Besides, it's still getting plenty of use with John."

"I think they certainly have everything they need, and then some," Wolf said with a short laugh.

Caroline poked him. "Hush."

They were silent for a moment, then Caroline asked softly, "Are you sorry we don't have kids?"

"No." Wolf's answer was immediate and sincere. "I've never felt the urge to have kids like a lot of men have, and as I've told you before, I like having you to myself. If that makes me selfish, so be it."

"You don't get asked by the others when you're having kids?"

"Nope. They know where I stand. And Ice, they're our friends, they couldn't give a shit if we have them or not, as long as we're happy."

"It's just that..."

Wolf squeezed Caroline. "I know. We've been over this. Screw society. I know many people don't think we're normal if we don't have kids. That we should be popping them out by now. But there's no rule book that says we have to have children if we don't want them. Besides, you're kept busy with everyone else's kids. I know you babysit every chance you get."

"I love them, but I also love being able to give them back."

Wolf smiled and kissed the top of Caroline's head. "Go to sleep, baby. You have to work in the morning, I've got PT, and then we have to survive the craziness that will be Brinique and Davisa's adoption party. I have a feeling you girls went overboard."

Caroline didn't answer, but Wolf felt her smile against him. Yup. They totally went overboard.

"Love you, Matthew."

"Love you too, Ice."

# Chapter Two

ALABAMA POWERS STOOD next to her friend, Summer Reed. Summer held her sleeping daughter, April, in her arms and they watched Brinique and Davisa screeching and jumping in the playhouse they'd rented for the party.

"They seem to be doing good," Summer said quietly.

"Yeah. For the most part they are," Alabama said easily. "Brinique sometimes still cries at night and Davisa has the occasional nightmare, but they've eased up a lot over the last few months."

"You've done an awesome thing, Alabama."

Alabama shrugged. "I've always wanted children, but growing up the way I did, I knew there were tons of kids out there who needed to be out of horrible home situations. Adoption is really the only way I want to have children."

"I love that Christopher didn't even blink when you told him you wanted to adopt."

Alabama smiled and looked over at her husband. He was standing by the bounce house watching his girls with a protective stance she knew would never really fade. "He didn't. I brought up fostering to him first, and he was a hundred percent in from the get-go. I know I've told you this already, but the very first call we got for placement was for Brinique and Davisa. Their mom was a drug addict and they were left to fend for themselves most of the time."

Alabama turned to Summer, getting worked up in her annoyance, repeating a story that Summer had heard many times. "When Child Protective Services showed up at their house for the first time, Brinique was only four and she was wearing a T-shirt of her mom's because she didn't have any clothes of her own. She stood over a naked Davisa and screeched, not letting the male officer get anywhere close to her." Alabama shuddered. "I can't stand to think about why, at *four*, Brinique felt she had to protect her three-year-old sister from a man."

Summer laid her hand on Alabama's shoulder. "Easy, girl. You've got them now. They're safe."

Alabama smiled at Summer and stated fiercely, "Yes, they are. And they're gonna stay that way."

The two women looked down at Davisa, who'd wandered over to where they were standing. She put her hand on Alabama's pants and tugged lightly. Alabama immediately kneeled down so she was eye level to her little girl. "Yes, sweetie?"

"Can I hold the baby?"

Alabama looked up at Summer, who smiled. "Of course. Come on, let's go sit over here."

The trio moved to a ring of chairs that had been set up. Alabama helped her daughter sit in one and Summer gently put April in Davisa's arms. "Hold on tight. I know she's only six months old, but she's heavy."

The women watched as the five-year-old carefully held the baby. Davisa didn't say anything for the longest time, she simply studied the infant carefully. Finally, she looked up in wonder. "She's so pale."

Summer supposed compared to Davisa, who had beautiful, warm chocolate-brown skin, April *was* very pale.

"Do you think my mommy would've wanted me if I was pale too?"

Alabama immediately kneeled down next to the little girl who was officially declared "hers" just that morning by the judge. Before she could speak, Abe was there.

He scooped up the little girl and the baby all together and sat in the chair and held the duo in his lap. Brinique had followed her dad over to the women and scooted up next to the chair as well. Summer stood back and watched one of her best friends in the world and her husband's teammate have a beautiful moment with their new daughters, feeling as if her heart would burst.

Abe put one arm around Brinique standing at his side and held his daughter to him, being careful not to jostle baby April. "Your birth mother didn't deserve you. And I'm not saying that to be mean, it's the truth. She had two of the most beautiful daughters on the planet, who she didn't take care of. She was selfish and only wanted to do what *she* wanted to do. Children are precious and parents have a responsibility to them to make sure they're fed, safe, and loved."

Abe looked his children in the eyes as he spoke. "You had a rough start to life, but you know what? You're a Powers now. You're mine. You're Alabama's, and you belong to every one of the men and women here today. We're one big family. You'll never be hungry again. You'll never be neglected again." He looked at Brinique. "You'll never have to worry about scary men coming into our house and hurting you or your sister. We love you. You're ours. Forever. I wouldn't care if your skin was purple or green or that it's darker than mine. It's what's inside that skin that I care about."

"What's inside our skin?" Davisa asked softly.

Without hesitation, Abe answered. "Your heart. Your blood. Your mind. You. *You* are inside your skin. And that's why I love you. And that's why Alabama loves you. And that's why everyone here loves you. Got it?"

"You won't send us back?" Brinique asked.

"No. You aren't ever going back."

"Even when we're bad?"

Alabama leaned in and touched Brinique's arm, picking up where her husband left off. "Baby, you'll never be bad. You might misbehave. You might do something that isn't right, but those are simply bad decisions. They don't make you a bad person. And the bottom line is that you're not going back. The judge today gave you to us forever. Your last name is now Powers. Just like mine. Just like Christopher's." She smiled at her daughter. "You're stuck with us now."

Brinique smiled hugely, showing off her crooked teeth. "I like being stuck with you guys."

"We like it too."

Davisa spoke up. "Does that mean we can call you Mommy and Daddy now?"

Alabama heard Summer sniff loudly from behind her, but she didn't look away from Davisa. This was perhaps one of the proudest moments in her life, no way was she missing a second of it. "You can call us whatever you're most comfortable with. Dad. Mom. Mommy. Daddy. Alabama. Abe. Christopher…whatever you want. But nothing would make me happier than having you call me your mom or mommy."

Davisa nodded solemnly and looked down at the

baby in her lap. "Okay. Mommy?"

"Yes, sweetheart?"

"I think the baby just pooped."

Alabama laughed, loving how she'd just had one of the most emotional conversations she'd ever had in her life, and Davisa could move on without blinking.

"How about I take her then?" Summer asked from behind them.

Davisa nodded and Summer leaned in and gathered April in her arms.

"Can we go play some more?"

"Of course, but be careful," Abe warned, helping Davisa off his lap.

"Okay, Daddy, we will," Brinique said brightly, before she and her sister ran off toward the bounce house again.

"Come here," Abe said to Alabama, pulling her into his lap.

Alabama settled in and sighed.

"You okay?"

She nodded. "Yeah, I know we've talked to them about what it means to be a foster kid and how we were working toward adopting them, but I didn't realize they still had doubts."

"Baby, hell, you had doubts when we met and you were an adult. They'll adjust. We just need to keep telling them that we love them for who they are. We need to make them feel safe…they'll be fine."

"I love you, Christopher."

"Love you too…now, when can we have cake?"

Alabama laughed and got off of her husband's lap. "Why are you always hungry?"

"Because my wife is insatiable and I need to keep my energy up to satisfy her?"

Alabama playfully slugged Christopher on the arm. "Whatever. Go watch your kids while I get the table ready."

Abe leaned over and picked her up until her feet dangled off the ground. "This has been one of the happiest days of my life. Besides the day you forgave me for being an ass, and our wedding, of course."

Alabama put her arms around his neck and kissed him, hard. "Me too. Now put me down. I have work to do."

CHEYENNE WADDLED OVER to where Summer was sitting with Fiona. Faulkner "Dude" Cooper, her very protective and attentive husband, had dropped her off before going to park the car.

"Hey, ladies."

"Hey, Cheyenne, you look ready to pop!"

"Don't I know it! Can you believe I have three more weeks to go?"

"It's crazy. Every time we hang out I'm ready to bend down and catch that baby before it can hit the ground," Summer teased.

"Hush. Don't say that around Faulkner. He's already super-protective. If he heard that, he wouldn't let me go anywhere. As it was, I had to beg to be able to come today."

"Beg?" Fiona asked with a raised eyebrow.

"Hush," Cheyenne said while blushing.

Fiona didn't hush. "Oh, I'm sure *that* was a hardship."

Cheyenne had shared with all the other women her husband's penchant to be dominant in the bedroom. But they all knew it worked well for the couple. "Yeah, well, I might have turned the tables on him a bit. He's...reluctant to go too far with me these days, so I use it to my advantage as much as I can."

Fiona laughed. "You are so in trouble once you have this baby and he can have his way with you again."

Cheyenne smiled widely. "I know. I can't wait."

"You okay? Need anything?" Faulkner had come up behind them while Cheyenne was getting settled into the chair.

"No, I'm good, hon. Thanks for dropping me off."

"Like I'd make you walk all the way from the parking lot. This place is packed. It's like Abe and Alabama invited the entire base!"

There were indeed lots and lots of people at the park. Kids were running everywhere and the happiness could almost be felt in the air.

"Yeah, well, those two precious girls deserve a huge party after everything they've been through," Cheyenne commented.

"Agreed. I'm going to go and find the guys. Are you sure you don't need anything?" Dude asked.

"I'm good. Fiona and Summer will take care of me."

Dude leaned down and kissed Cheyenne, a bit longer and more inappropriately than the surroundings and company would merit, but Fiona and Summer were used to it. When he wandered off looking for his teammates, Summer adjusted April in her arms and sighed. "It seems like I'm always blushing when I'm around the two of you."

Cheyenne laughed. "Me too."

"How's April doing?" Fiona asked, leaning over and peering down at the still sleeping infant. "Is she sleeping better?"

"Yeah, she can go almost all night now, thank God. When we first brought her home, every time she moved Sam was up checking on her. As much as I'll miss the times when he brings her to me and watches fascinated as I breastfeed her, I'm looking forward to sleeping through the night again."

"I can't believe you agreed to name her April."

Summer sighed. I know. "Sam loves my name, even though I sometimes think it's ridiculous, but he was so proud of himself for thinking up the name April. I mean, I know her birthday is in April, but it still seems silly."

"It's not silly," Mozart said from behind them. All three women jumped in surprise.

"Jeez, Sam, don't sneak up on us!"

"I didn't sneak, I walked up just like everyone else does."

"No, you sneak. You SEALs think you're walking normally, but it's ingrained in you to be quiet and silent when you move. One of these days I'm putting a bell on you."

Mozart only smiled. "As I said, April's name isn't silly. It's beautiful, just like her mom. Now you and her have something in common. You were named after when you were born. I love it, and I love you."

Summer tilted her head up and was rewarded with a kiss from her husband.

"Can I get you anything?"

"No, I'm good. Thanks. Can you see if you can find Jess and Kason though? I know those two babies of hers are probably slowing them down. I want to make sure she gets to rest when she gets here," Summer commented.

"Will do. I'll send them over as soon as I track them

down. Love you."

"Love you too, Sam."

The women watched as Sam "Mozart" Reed walked away.

"He's as good looking from the back as he is from the front," Fiona commented dryly.

Everyone laughed.

"How are you healing? Are you really all good now?" Fiona asked. "April certainly did a number on your body."

"Yeah, having that many stitches down there wasn't fun, but I'm good. This will be our only baby though. I'm almost forty and while I love her, Sam doesn't want to put my body through that again, and I can't say I disagree. I also want to be able to raise her and then kick her out to go to college when she's eighteen so Sam and I can enjoy our retirement…you know?"

"Yeah, makes sense," Cheyenne agreed immediately. "Faulkner and I want lots of babies after this one, but I know I might change my mind once she's actually here. But I'm also not even thirty yet, so I have lots of time to decide to have more, or to dissuade Faulkner."

"Yo! How about some help here?"

Fiona immediately got up and waved off Cheyenne and Summer. "I got this. Stay put." She hurried over to the duo. Jessyka was loaded down with one-year-old John in her arms and a bag over her right shoulder.

Kason was walking next to her with their daughter in his arms and another, bigger bag over *his* shoulder.

Fiona went straight for Sara, the two-year-old, who was thankfully sleeping in her dad's arms.

Jess was used to her friends wanting to get their hands on her kids rather than being more practical and helping her with what seemed like the ten bags she was always carrying. It didn't bother her, she was happy they all shared her love for her kids. "I finally got her out of the house after two temper tantrums because she first wanted to wear her princess dress…the dress she wore at your wedding, Cheyenne," Jess said as they arrived at the little group, "and then because she wanted to wear her plastic play-dress-up shoes instead of her sandals. She's going to make me gray before my time."

"She's a little angel, how can you say that?"

Kason dropped the bag on the ground next to an empty chair. "You got this, babe?"

Jess leaned up and wrapped her free arm around Kason. "I got this. Go on, go have fun with your friends. Be good."

Benny shook his head and rolled his eyes at his wife. "I'll be back to check on you in a bit. Don't let her sleep too long, she needs to run off some of her energy if we want to sleep at all tonight." He leaned in close to Jess, "I have plans for later, and I don't want to be interrupted by a toddler who can't sleep because she's too excited."

Jess blushed, glancing at her friends to see if they'd heard her husband's words. Seeing they were cooing over her kids, but smiling, she realized they'd heard every word her husband had said. Knowing they were happy for her, she nevertheless whispered back at Kason, trying to keep her friends from hearing *everything*, "Don't worry, I'll make sure she's up in a bit. I like it when you have plans. Love you."

Kason kissed Jess hard, then stepped back. "Love you too."

Jessyka settled down into an empty chair and watched as Kason sauntered away toward his teammates, and then smiled as her three friends settled into the chairs beside her.

Soon, Caroline and Alabama wandered over to join the little group. They pulled up chairs and sat in a semi-circle, watching the kids play in the bounce house and the other equipment in the park.

"I freaking love this," Fiona announced.

"What?"

"This. Us. Being here. Holding babies. Watching the kids play. Watching our husbands talk about who knows what manly shit they're talking about. We are six lucky women, that's for sure."

Everyone nodded.

"Five and a half kids, six husbands, six friends."

"Five and a half?" Caroline questioned.

Fiona gestured toward Cheyenne's protruding belly. "Yeah, I'm counting Cheyenne's baby as a half until she's born. Until Cheyenne has to change diapers, it's only a half."

Cheyenne laughed at her friend. "You know what's missing?"

"What?" Fiona asked.

"Tex and Melody."

"True. We should totally Skype them while we're here," Caroline proclaimed.

"Oh, hell yeah. That'll be awesome. I haven't seen her and Akilah in too long!" Fiona chimed in.

"How's Akilah doing?" Cheyenne asked.

"Last I heard from Melody, she was great. She had the amputation, and Tex is teaching her the ropes on how to take care of her stump and how the prosthetic works," Caroline told the group.

"Does she miss Iraq?"

"I don't think so. Tex and Melody have done a great job in making sure they cook her familiar foods, and they've even found a support group there in Pittsburgh so she can talk to and be friends with other girls displaced from Iraq."

"Did they ever find her parents?" Alabama asked.

Caroline shook her head sadly. "Akilah says they were killed, and Tex doesn't think she's lying about it.

She was lucky the United Nations doctor over in Baghdad felt sorry for her and pulled strings to get her seen back here in the States. Contacting Tex and letting him know her story was the best thing that ever happened to her."

"How's she doing in school?" Summer asked.

"Melody says she's still struggling with English a bit, but she gets better every day. It's hard enough being twelve years old, but to be twelve in a new country, learning the language, *and* dealing with a major injury and how to get about in daily life with only one arm…well, Melody is amazed at how well she's doing."

"We are *so* Skyping them today!" Alabama announced resolutely.

After chatting for a bit longer, Sara finally woke up and Fiona put her down and all the women watched the little two-year-old toddle off to play with a group of kids in a big sandbox nearby. Jess waved at one of the other mothers from the base, who motioned that she'd watch the little girl.

The group sat around talking about feeding, toddlers, childbirth and other random topics until one by one their husbands came over. Wolf and Mozart pulled up chairs next to their wives, Dude stood behind Cheyenne and rubbed her shoulders. Benny and Cookie sat on the ground next to their wives, and Abe scooped Alabama out of her chair and sat in it, with his wife on his lap. Brinique and Davisa wandered back over, finally tired from running around, and sat next to their new mom and dad.

"Thank you all for coming out today," Alabama told everyone. "It means more than you'll ever know. I'm proud of us. I have two children who I helped take out of a horrible situation, much as I had growing up. Jess, you and Kason got right to work and started popping out babies right after you were married. The house you guys bought out in the countryside is beautiful, and after Kason finishes fixing it up, it's going to be even better. Fiona, you've come a long way from where you were after Hunter found you."

"Well, I've had a lot of therapy," Fiona said honestly. "And a lot of help from my friends."

Everyone nodded in agreement and Alabama continued. "Cheyenne, you're the most beautiful pregnant woman I've ever seen. And I swear if you didn't tell me the doctor had most definitely said there was only one baby in there, I'd think you were having triplets."

"Shut your mouth, evil woman," Cheyenne teased. They all laughed at the gleam in Faulkner's eyes.

"Looks like Faulkner wouldn't mind, though."

"Yeah, well, *he* doesn't have to squeeze them out his—"

Alabama interrupted Cheyenne, gesturing toward Brinique and Davisa in warning as she did. "And

Summer, I'm so proud of you for getting that HR Director job. I know you weren't sure you wanted to get back into the field, but the small-company thing is working for you. And April is beautiful as well."

Alabama took a deep breath and turned to Caroline. "And Caroline. What would all of us have done without you? Seriously. You're our leader. You took us in and cared for us from the get-go."

"Well, except for warning me off Faulkner," Cheyenne said with a laugh.

"You and Matthew might not have any kids, but why do I feel sometimes as if we're *all* your kids? You're there when we have questions and worries. You've looked after John when he was colicky and Jess didn't know what to do anymore. You babysit Brinique and Davisa whenever I ask, without question. You make sure Tex, Melody, and Akilah are always included and invited when we do things. You're the glue that holds us all together when our men go off to save the world. I love you more than I can ever say. Thank you for being you, and for being our friend."

Wolf, Abe, Cookie, Mozart, Dude, and Benny all rolled their eyes at each other good naturedly when their wives all started crying. They might be tough-as-nails women who wouldn't let them get away with any crap, but with the pregnancy hormones and general happiness they all felt at the moment, it seemed as if they could all cry at the drop of a hat.

"I thought Mommy was happy?" Davisa said in confusion in a too-loud whisper to Christopher.

Everyone laughed at the five-year-old's innocent statement and wiped their eyes.

"We are happy, baby. But sometimes people cry happy tears," Alabama tried to explain.

"Grownups are weird," Brinique explained to her sister. "Can we go play some more?"

Abe palmed his daughter's head. "Yes. Be careful though."

"We will. Come on, Davisa, race you to the monkey bars!"

The two girls ran away from the group shrieking with laughter.

"This is one of the best days of my life," Cheyenne declared. "Friends, kids, and the love of my life by my side. What else could we ask for?"

Everyone agreed wholeheartedly.

Each of the twelve people in the close-knit group would remember this day and the joy and love surrounding it in the upcoming weeks, needing the memories to keep them going.

# Chapter Three

*Sergeant Penelope Turner was once again seen on a videotape provided by ISIS. Turner has been missing for six weeks now. This video was the longest one of the kidnapped American soldier to date. She is seen sitting in what seems to be a tent and reading from a long-winded, rambling letter that extols Allah and claims, among other things, that there will be more killing and deaths if the Americans don't stop sending soldiers to the Middle East.*

*She reads the letter in a monotone voice, and doesn't look up at the camera at all. She only looks up after a voice is heard reprimanding her in the background. Analysts have concluded that Turner looks like she has lost some weight, but she is still remarkably healthy, all things considered.*

*There has been no word from the President about what, if any, rescue attempts are in the works for this brave American soldier. Her family continues to push for information and for the government to make some sort of gesture to gain her freedom.*

*The official response is that the United States does not negotiate with terrorists.*

*More information at the ten o'clock hour.*

CHEYENNE SAT ON the couch with Faulkner and held his hand firmly.

"We're leaving in the morning."

"But—"

Dude hauled Cheyenne into his arms and held her as tightly as he could with her enormous belly hampering his efforts. "I don't want to go. Dammit, I don't want to go. I even asked Commander Hurt if I could sit this one out, and was denied."

"Really?"

Dude nodded. "Yeah. Which means every single one of us is needed for this mission. I won't lie to you, baby. I have a bad feeling about it. I don't know if it's because I have to leave you here, about to have my baby, or if it's because of the mission itself. But mark my words. *Nothing* is going to keep me from getting back here to you and our little one. Nothing. Got it?"

Cheyenne nodded and sniffed. She'd always tried to be brave when Faulkner had to leave, but this time was different. They'd practiced breathing techniques together, he'd gone to every doctor appointment with her. He hadn't missed one step of her pregnancy. The thought of her husband missing the actual birth of their daughter made her feel empty inside.

"Words, Shy."

She smiled at that. He hadn't changed in the two years since they'd met. He was still as bossy as ever. "Yeah. I got it."

"Your only job is to stay safe. Keep our daughter safe. You've got all the girls here to keep you busy. If, God forbid, I miss the birth of our daughter, make sure you get someone to film it for me."

"What?" They hadn't talked about that at all. "I'm not filming it. Gross!"

"Shy, I've waited my entire life for this moment. To watch my child being born is not gross, it's fucking beautiful."

"But, Faulkner—"

"Please."

Well shit. He'd said please. *She* was usually the one begging, not him. She nodded reluctantly. "Okay, but we are not breaking out the video of my cooter to show off to anyone else. Ever."

Dude only smiled. Double shit. He sobered and said in a gruff tone, "And if your so-called family dares to show their faces at the hospital or try to insinuate they should be allowed to see my daughter, sic Caroline on them."

Cheyenne smiled, remembering the last time Faulkner had "sicced" Caroline on her mom and sister. They'd shown up at *Aces Bar and Grill* while they were eating, and Caroline had headed them off before they'd even gotten close to their table. Cheyenne didn't know exactly why they'd come to see her, Caroline wouldn't really tell her, but they'd probably wanted something from her.

Caroline had gone off on her family. Cheyenne hadn't even *heard* of some of the insults she'd hurled at them. Faulkner had kept his eyes on the trio, but hadn't moved while Caroline was giving them hell. It wasn't like him to not take the opportunity to tell her family how much he didn't respect or like them, but he'd told her later that Caroline had been doing such a great job at dressing them down, he didn't feel the need to join in.

Cheyenne answered Faulkner, "I will, although I don't think they'll show up. I think they finally got the hint when you returned their Christmas card unopened with the words, 'You don't exist for Cheyenne anymore,' scrawled on the back."

Dude leaned down and buried his face in his wife's hair and rested his hand on her swollen belly, not addressing her comment about the stupid Christmas card, but instead saying what was foremost on his mind. "I love you, Shy. And I love our daughter. I don't know what I'd do without you in my life. You take me as I am. You're my match in every way. I'm dying inside thinking I might not be around for one of the most important days in our lives."

Cheyenne held on to Faulkner, knowing she had to reassure him. "Even if you don't get back for her birth, this is only the start of this child's life. Even if you miss the big events, you'll be there in the middle of the night when she needs changing. You'll be there when she has a nightmare. You'll chase the boogeyman out of the closet for her. You'll take her for ice cream and let her cry on your shoulder when she falls down. You'll teach her to ride a bicycle. You'll be there giving the evil eye to her first date. You'll be there for her everyday life. Missing events here and there doesn't matter. It's being there for the everyday, boring things that she'll remember most and that are important. Yeah?"

"Fuck, I love you."

Cheyenne smiled. "I love you too. Should we talk about names again?" She hated to bring it up, as they usually ended up arguing about it, but if Faulkner had a feeling he might not make it home for her birth, they'd better talk about it now.

"No, I don't want to jinx it. If we decide now, I *know* I won't make it home in time."

Cheyenne smiled at him in exasperation. "But if you don't make it home, I'll have to name her without you. I don't want you to be disappointed."

"We've talked about this enough, Shy, you know what I like and what I don't. *If* I don't get back, I trust you to give our daughter a name she won't get made fun of for the rest of her life and that she won't want to change as soon as she's old enough to think for herself. Now, if we're done with this conversation, I need to show my daughter who her daddy is one more time."

"Jeez, Faulkner, I swear you're hornier now when I'm as big as a house than you were when we first got married."

"I can't help it. You're just so fucking beautiful with my child inside you, I can't get enough."

Cheyenne let Faulkner help her off the couch—lord knew she had trouble getting out of it on her own nowadays—and lead her into their bedroom. There, he proceeded to strip her out of her nightgown and he spent the next few hours worshiping her body and showing her in every way he could how much she meant to him. He loved her as if it might be the last time he'd ever get to love her.

"YOU'VE GOT YOUR tracking thing, right?" Jessyka asked Kason nervously for the third time that night after they'd put the kids to bed.

"I've got it. Don't worry."

"I can't not worry. Every time you step out of the

house, I worry."

"I know, and that's one of the four hundred and thirty-three reasons why I love you."

"Only four hundred and thirty-three?"

"Come here, Jess." Benny hauled his wife into his arms. "We get called away on missions a lot. Why are you so worried?"

"I don't know. I just have a feeling this time is different."

Benny didn't say anything, because he had the same feeling. He changed the subject. "Are you all set with John and Sara? Will you be able to do your volunteering thing at the youth center without me to help with them?"

"Yeah, Caroline said we could come and stay there for a few nights and Fiona said the same thing. I can go and volunteer while they're looking after the kids."

"I hate that you don't feel comfortable being out here in our house when I'm not here."

Jess tried to explain. "It's not that I don't feel comfortable, but you do a lot, and you don't even realize it, I don't think. With John and Sara being so close in age, and John just now starting to walk and Sara needing lots of attention, it's just easier for me to have help."

Seeing the dismayed look on her husband's face, Jess hurried to reassure him. "I'm not saying this to make you feel guilty. Single parents do it by themselves all the time, and I have a newfound respect for all the men and women out in the world who are raising their kids on their own. Caroline and Fiona have offered to be that help. That's all."

"Okay, Jess. I'll let it go. I'll be back as soon as I can and I'll work even harder to get the house finished up so you'll feel more comfortable here. Maybe we can look into getting some help around the house. A nanny or something. I don't want you to lose yourself either. I know how important volunteering at the youth center is. It's your way of helping kids like Tabitha.

Jess sighed as she thought of the young girl she'd loved, but ultimately couldn't help.

"Yeah, I can't help but think that if Tabitha had had some sort of safe place to go after school, maybe she wouldn't have felt so isolated and maybe she would've spoken up about the abuse she was going through."

"I'm proud of you, Jess. You could be bitter or depressed over what happened to Tabitha, but you aren't. You turned the experience around and used it to fuel your desire to help other teenagers."

"You're the best husband ever, Kason. Don't forget it." Jess smiled at him. She loved him so much and had no idea what she'd done to get so lucky to have him in her life, but she wasn't going to look a gift horse in the mouth. She wasn't letting him go. Ever.

"I won't, but if you feel like showing me how great I

am before I go…I wouldn't be opposed."

Jess giggled and stepped back from him and pointed over his shoulder. "What is *that*?"

When he turned to look, Jessyka smiled and hurried out of the room toward their bedroom as fast as her body would take her. She threw her words over her shoulder as she made her way down the hall. "Ha! Made you look! First one in the bedroom gets to be on top!"

"Why, you little sneak!" Benny said with no heat. He came after her, but made sure to let Jess stay in front of him. He liked her on top as much as she liked being there. Her limp, a result of one leg being shorter than the other, didn't really slow her down, but they both knew if he really wanted to, he could overtake her in a second. Watching his wife's sexy ass sway as she fast-walked down the hall to their bedroom never failed to make him smile.

Later that night, Benny knew he'd never forget the look on Jess's face as she rode him. Her head thrown back, her long black hair brushing against his thighs, and the smile on her face. It was pure gold, and she was all his.

MOZART SAT IN the rocking chair holding his six-month-old daughter and looking down at her in awe. She was the most amazing thing he'd ever seen. He wasn't a sappy man. He'd lived a hard life and never expected to have a wife, never mind a daughter. One of his favorite things ever was watching as April breastfed from Summer. His girls. They were so beautiful it made his heart hurt.

April had woken up a bit ago. She was doing better at sleeping through the night, but still had times where she'd wake up, and he'd fetched her and brought her to Summer. Summer had only been half awake and Mozart had helped April latch on to his wife's nipple and he'd held his daughter to his wife's breast as she nursed. Summer had smiled tiredly at him, and palmed his face when April had finished.

"Thank you, Sam. I love you."

"Shhh, you're welcome. I love you too. Go back to sleep. I'll be back."

Now he was sitting in April's room. His daughter had fallen back to sleep a while ago, but he was enjoying breathing in her baby scent and holding her in his arms. She was growing up so fast and he could suddenly envision her as a teenager, not wanting her dad to hug her. In the back of his mind, Mozart tried to tamp down the worry he had about the mission they were about to go on. Even though they'd been on many missions similar to this one, somehow he knew this one would be different.

Summer found Sam in their baby's room, rocking

her and watching her sleep. "You didn't come back," she said softly, not wanting to disturb her daughter.

Mozart looked up at his beautiful wife. Her blonde hair was in disarray around her face and her blue eyes were sleepy. She'd thrown on one of his shirts that he'd inevitably left on the floor and was holding it closed around her body with her arms crossed in front of her. His heart felt as if it was going to burst with love for her. He'd come so close to losing her two years ago, and there wasn't a day that went by that he didn't thank God the team had gotten to her in time.

"Hey. Sorry. Can you believe we've had her in our lives for six months already? You never know what you're missing until you have it in the first place."

"Like you."

"What?"

"Like you. I never knew I was missing you, until I *had* you."

"Come here, Sunshine."

Summer padded over to her husband and kneeled on the carpet next to the chair. She palmed his scarred cheek and ran her thumb over his lips. "Even if we'd never had April, my life would've been completely full. April isn't a culmination of our love. I love you, Sam Reed."

"You'll never know how glad I am that you stood up for me that day up at Big Bear. By some miracle you don't see my flaws, and I'm not only talking about the scar on my cheek. I love you too, Sunshine. You and April are the most important things in my life. I'll move heaven and earth to always come home to you."

"I know you will. Come to bed, hon."

Mozart nodded and stood up, careful not to jostle his little girl. He lay her gently in her crib and kissed her on the top of her head, her fuzzy hair soft against his lips. He put his hand on her back, amazed at how tiny she still was. He could cover her entire back with the palm of one hand. "Rest easy, Angel. Daddy loves you."

Summer took Sam's hand and led him back to their bedroom. She stripped him of his flannel pants and took her time showing him just how much he was loved.

Later, when they were dozing off—Summer after having come several times, and Mozart after finally allowing himself to release inside the love of his life—he heard her say softly and groggily in his ear, "Rest easy, Sam. I love you."

COOKIE SAT ACROSS from Fiona at the table as they ate. "Are you sure you're going to be okay while I'm gone?"

Fiona smiled at Hunter, not getting irritated with him, knowing he asked out of love. "For the tenth time, yes, hon, I'll be fine. I haven't had a flashback in a couple of months now."

"I know, but—"

"I understand that you get nervous every time you leave because of what happened two years ago when you were on that mission, but I *swear* I've got the tracker on, and I'll call Caroline or Tex if I start to feel weird. I'm not going to run off like I did before. I'm much better now. You've made sure of that."

Cookie pushed his mostly empty plate away and put his elbows on the table and leaned toward Fiona. "I just worry about you."

"I know, and I love you for it. You worry about me just like I worry about you. You about done?"

Cookie nodded and watched as Fiona took his plate to the sink. He stood up and opened the dishwasher and took the dishes after Fiona rinsed them, placing them into the machine. They worked in tandem, without words, just as they had many nights before.

The kitchen was clean and the dishes were done. "Want to take a bath?"

Fiona looked at her husband. Something was off about him, but she wasn't sure what. "Sure. You going to join me?"

He shook his head. "Not tonight. I just want to pamper you."

Fiona nodded.

"Okay, give me a few minutes, and I'll go get it started for you."

"I can do it."

"I know, but I want to."

"All right. I'll find a book to read and join you in a few."

Fiona watched Hunter walk down the hall to their bedroom. She cocked her head, trying to figure out what his deal was. He was usually protective of her, especially before he left for a mission, but this was new. He'd drawn her a bath before, but tonight it somehow felt different. In the past he'd make love to her as if it would be the last time they'd ever be together, *then* give her the lecture about being safe and asking if she'd be okay. He didn't usually delay going to bed with a bath for her first.

Fiona grabbed a romance novel off the shelf, one of her favorites, and headed to their bedroom. She could hear the water running into the tub, but didn't expect the candles when she entered their large bathroom. Hunter had lit as many as he could find, not caring that they were all different scents and the smell would probably give them both a headache later. It was simply beautiful.

He didn't say much, but watched as she stripped out of her clothes and climbed into the tub.

"Is the temperature okay?"

"Scalding hot…so it's perfect."

Hunter smiled at her. "Okay, I'll be back in twenty

minutes or so to check on you."

Fiona nodded and again worried as she watched him leave. Something was bothering him and she had to get him to fess up before the night was over.

After her bath, and after Hunter had dried every inch of her skin, and after he'd bent her over their mattress and had taken her from behind—quite thoroughly and satisfyingly—and after they'd snuggled down into the soft pillowy mattress, Fiona asked the question that had been nagging at her all night.

"What's up, Hunter?"

"What do you mean?"

"I mean, you've never been quite so…caring—before you've left before."

He was silent so long, Fiona wondered if he was going to answer her at all…indeed if he was still awake.

"I know I'm not supposed to admit it, but this one worries me."

Trying not to tense up, Fiona asked him why.

"You know I can't tell you where I'm going, but I could be gone for a while. I'm worried about you. I'm worried about the other women. I'm worried about their kids. I'm just worried in general."

A little alarmed, as it wasn't like Hunter to be this concerned about anything—he usually had a kick-butt-and-take-no-prisoners attitude—Fiona tried to reassure him. "I can't ask you not to be worried. Hell, if you told me not to be concerned about *you*, I'd laugh in your face. But I'll be okay. The girls will be okay. Everyone will be just fine. We look after each other when you guys are gone, just as you all have each other's backs when you're on a mission. Trust in us to keep on keepin' on while you're all gone. No matter what, this is our family. We might not have any kids, but I'd do anything for John, Sara, Brinique, Davisa, April and the as-of-yet-unnamed baby Cooper."

"Just promise me…*promise me*, if I don't come home, you'll take care of yourself. I can't stand to think of you as lost and alone and broken as you were when I found you two years ago when you'd run north."

Wanting to comment on the "not coming home" part, and break out in tears, Fiona held them back. She needed to be a rock for Hunter. He needed her to be strong. "I promise."

Cookie nodded because he couldn't say anything through the knot in his throat, and wrapped his arms around Fiona as tightly as he thought she could stand. He hitched one leg over her hip and surrounded himself in her scent and her body. If this was the last time he'd be able to hold her, as his gut was screaming at him it possibly could be, he wanted to imprint himself onto her.

He felt the second Fiona fell asleep in his arms. They'd both ignored the tears that leaked out of her eyes as they held each other. Cookie didn't sleep even a minute. He wanted to cherish every last second with the love of his life in his arms.

ALABAMA AND CHRISTOPHER sat on the couch next to each other, each with a little girl on their lap, explaining that Daddy was leaving on another trip. Over the last year and a half that Brinique and Davisa been living with them, they'd slowly understood more and more about what it was Daddy did.

"When will you be back?" Brinique asked tearfully.

"I'm not sure, pumpkin," Abe told his daughter, wiping away the tears that made streaks down her little face. "But I *will* be back."

"My other daddy left and never came back," Davisa said matter-of-factly. Alabama knew she'd never known who her real father was, her birth mother probably never knew either, but Davisa had most likely heard the woman complaining that the man had left without a backward glance anyway.

"He might have left, but I'll do everything in my power to get back," Christopher promised. "Do you think I'd leave three such beautiful women forever? Not if I can help it. I love you all too much. No matter what happens in your life, you need to know that your mom and I love you very much. We *picked* you. A lot of other mommies and daddies don't get a choice in their children. We had a choice and we choose you guys. Don't ever forget it."

Brinique sat up straight in Christopher's lap. "Yeah. You picked us. Out of all the little boys and girls who needed a home. You picked *us*."

Abe nodded and repeated the words Brinique obviously wanted to hear. "That's right, little one. We chose you. So even though I'm leaving, I'm not leaving because of anything you did. It's my job. It's what I do."

"Mommy said you're one of the good guys. You go out into the world and put the bad people in jail."

Abe looked over at Alabama and winked. "Well, yeah, sorta, but that's the basics."

"Where's the world?"

"What do you mean, sweetie?"

"You go out into the world...where's the world?"

"Ah." Abe shifted in his seat, snuggling Brinique closer to his chest as he did. "The world is anywhere other than where we are right now." He tried to keep it simple for his six-year-old.

"So, will you be in another state?"

Alabama knew this was getting trickier now. She knew Abe couldn't tell anyone where they were going, not even his precocious little girl. She stepped in. "We don't know where Daddy will be, but Uncle Hunter and all your other uncles will take care of him for us until he can get back home."

"But Super Tex will know where you are, right? Mommy, you said Uncle Tex always knows where everyone is 'cos he's tacking them and that makes him kinda like a super hero…right?"

Alabama tried not to wince. Obviously Davisa was smarter than the average five-year-old. She remembered every single thing she was told. "*Tracking*, not tacking, and yes, Uncle Tex will know."

"Okay then. As long as Daddy doesn't get lost and can find his way back home, it's good. Will you read us a story tonight, Daddy?"

Alabama wished she could turn off her worry as easily as her daughters seemed to be able to. She and Christopher helped the girls get ready for bed and tucked them in. They still slept in the same room, feeling more comfortable being together, even after a year and a half away from their horrible birth mother. Christopher read a bedtime story and the girls were out before he'd reached page six.

They both kissed their cheeks and Abe whispered what he told them every night whether they were asleep or awake. "The sooner you go to sleep, the sooner a new day will come." They stood in the doorway for a long moment.

"They're beautiful kids, Alabama. I'm so proud of you for taking the initiative and pushing me to accept the foster placement. I can't even imagine our life without them in it, and I don't want to."

"Does it bother you when they call us Mom and Dad in public and people look twice?"

"Because we're white and they're black? Fuck no. Let people say whatever they want. Those girls are *mine.*"

God, Alabama loved this man.

Abe eased the girls' door closed, leaving it open a crack so they could hear either of them if they needed them in the night, and they went across the hall to their bedroom. They'd had to be creative and careful whenever they'd made love in the past year. Neither wanted their kids walking in on something they shouldn't be seeing.

Abe made easy, sweet love to Alabama, making sure they were both quiet as they climaxed. He pulled Alabama on top of him and felt her relax, boneless, into him. He knew they had to get up and put something on, just in case the girls came wandering into their room, but at the moment he didn't want to move. The feel of Alabama's smooth skin against his was as close as he'd get to heaven here on earth.

"I'm going to miss you." Alabama's voice was muted and heartfelt.

"I'm going to miss you too."

Alabama knew she couldn't demand Christopher

promise to come back to her, but she wanted to.

"Do me a favor?"

"Anything," Alabama told her husband honestly.

"Don't accept any more foster placements until I get back."

Alabama pushed herself up on Christopher's chest until she could just see him in the low light of the room. "What?"

"I know you. You'll get anxious, and you'll worry while I'm gone. I know you deal with stress better if you're busy. So I figure if asked, you'd gladly take on another child in need. When we take in another foster, I want to be here. I want to help him or her acclimate. And I can't do that if you're here by yourself."

Alabama relaxed into Christopher. For a second she'd thought he didn't want to adopt any more kids. Yes, they'd talked about it, and agreed they both wanted a large family of adopted kids, but she'd jumped to conclusions. She loved him all the more for wanting to be a part of every potential foster they had. "Okay, I can do that."

"If something happens to me—"

"No. Nothing will happen to you," Alabama butted in.

Abe continued as if she hadn't interrupted. "If something happens to me, I still want you to have the large family you've always dreamed about. Don't let it stop you."

Alabama's breath hitched in her chest. "I won't," she got out, and buried her face in the space between his shoulder and his face. She felt Christopher's hand wrap around the back of her neck.

"I worry about you from the moment I get up in the morning to the second I fall asleep. I might be away on a mission, and I might be a hundred percent focused on that mission, but you're always there, in the back of my mind. I know you're here, with our kids, waiting on me, and it makes me more determined than ever to get back to you. I know there's always a risk that one day that stubbornness on my part might not be enough, and I want you to reach for your dreams, whether I'm standing next to you cheering you on or not. Okay?"

"Okay," Alabama told him through her watery tears, not able to rebut his comments. They were beautiful and heartbreaking all at the same time.

"Sleep now, sweetheart. The sooner you sleep, the sooner I'll be home."

CAROLINE STOOD AT the door of the house looking out into the dark yard. Matthew stood behind her with his arms around her waist, holding her against his chest. They stood without talking for a long while. Finally, Caroline broke the silence.

"You're being sent in to try to rescue that girl, aren't you?"

Wolf didn't answer, and Caroline sighed. She turned in her husband's embrace and looped her arms around his neck as she gazed up at him. He looked down at her with such love and patience, she almost couldn't stand it.

"I know, you can't tell me, but in my gut I know that's where you guys are going. Don't worry, I won't say anything to the others, but can I just say one thing before I drop it?" Caroline knew Matthew was uncomfortable with the conversation, but he'd never admit it.

"Of course, Ice. Say whatever you need."

"You'll get her out. You'll find her, kill those assholes, and get her home. I *know* it."

At that, she saw Matthew's lips quirk upward. "You do, huh?"

"Yeah. You guys wouldn't rest until I was home and safe, and you didn't really even know me then either. This woman has *got* to be tough as hell. If she's been held for as long as the TV reporters say she has, she has to be."

"Ice—" Wolf began, but Caroline talked over him.

"I'm over what happened to me, we've talked about it, and I spoke to that therapist last year when I started having those nightmares, but there's something about this woman that gets to me. I heard her brother's interview with that talk-show host the other night. She joined the Army Reserves because she wanted to serve her country on a larger scale than being a firefighter did. Her brother says she's an excellent firefighter. She's worked her butt off and all the guys respect the hell out of her. She can make it through this, she's just waiting for some help. And who better to help her than you? And Hunter, Christopher, Sam, Faulkner, and Kason? You guys have all helped your women get out of shitty situations, so I know this will be no different. But please, do me a favor, Matthew."

"What's that, Ice?"

Caroline noticed he was careful to neither confirm nor deny where the team was going.

"This Penelope Turner is someone's sister. She's someone's daughter and friend. She's just like me. Or Fiona, or any of the others. I know I don't have to tell you to do whatever you have to in order to get her out of there…because I know you will. She's suffered enough and she needs to come home."

Wolf leaned down and gathered his wife to his chest. Fuck, he loved this woman. She could be railing at him to be careful, or crying because she was upset. Instead she'd already taken an unknown woman under her wing as if she was a part of her posse. She had more love inside her than any other woman he'd ever known.

"Okay, Ice." It was as close as he'd ever come to

breaking his top-secret government clearance.

He felt Caroline nod against his chest. She obviously knew he was uneasy with his words because she immediately changed the subject.

"All right then. Come on. You're leaving in the morning. It's time for you to make love to your wife."

Wolf grinned. "Yes, ma'am."

ON THE OTHER side of the country, Melody woke and saw that Tex hadn't joined her in their bed yet. She yawned and swung her feet over the side of the mattress, disturbing Baby in the process. But the dog didn't move other than to lift her head, sigh, and plop it down to go back to sleep.

Grinning at her lazy dog, but thankful she was still around to *be* lazy, Melody grabbed her ratty robe that was more comfortable than anything she'd ever worn, and sauntered out into the hall to find her husband.

Looking into the living room but not seeing him, and ignoring the mess that inevitably came from having an almost-teenager in the house, Melody went down into the basement to Tex's safe-room office. He'd set it up because of the extra security his computers warranted, and also, in his words, just in case they needed it for protection.

She pushed open the door Tex had left ajar, knowing she'd probably miss him in their bed and come looking for him. Melody saw her husband sitting at his desk fiddling with the mouse. She came up behind him and buried her face in his neck, giving him a chance to blacken the screen if there was something on there he didn't want her to see.

She'd learned over the last year and a half to let him have the privacy he needed. She didn't want to know half the stuff he did. She was better off *not* knowing.

"Everything okay?"

"Hummmm."

Okaaaay, that meant no. "The team?"

"They leave in the morning for a mission."

Melody waited.

"It's not going to be good."

Melody wasn't sure what to say. Tex helped lots of Special Forces teams across the country. She figured he meant the SEAL team from California since he didn't specify which team…since she was closest to them. Wolf and his team, and their wives and children, meant the world to them both, and hearing that the guys would be headed out on a mission that was "not going to be good" was very bad indeed.

"What can I do?"

Tex turned in his chair, grabbed Melody and pulled her so she had no choice but to straddle him. Her legs bent at the knees and fit into the spaces by his hips on the chair. He pulled her into him until they were groin to groin and chest to chest. He slowly undid the knot of the belt on the robe and pulled it open. He knew she'd be naked underneath. She liked to sleep that way as much as he enjoyed finding her that way when he joined her in bed.

He slipped his hands around her waist and buried his face in her cleavage. Tex felt Melody's hand clasp the back of his head as she held him to her.

"I love you. I love that you don't ask questions, but the first thing you say is 'what can I do?' I love that you miss me enough when I don't come to bed that you come looking for me. I love that you didn't even flinch when I said I wanted to adopt a handicapped, pre-adolescent girl from Iraq that I'd never even met. Most of all, I just love you. Every last inch of you. And to answer your question, there's nothing we can really do. Just wait and pray. You might call the girls a bit more, and if you feel up for it, you might even take a trip out there."

"Can you come too? I know they'd love to see you."

Tex shook his head. "I'd love to see them, but I need to be here. Watching. Waiting. I want to be here with my computers and servers in case they need me. And I have a bad feeling they *will* need me."

"Oh, Tex. You aren't Superman, no matter what Alabama's daughters call you."

"I know, but the hair on the back of my neck is sticking up and I'm certain they're gonna need my help where they're going."

Melody studied her husband. They'd taken a very long vacation after an ex-classmate, Diane, had been arrested for stalking her. They'd driven out with Baby to Las Vegas and gotten married, just as they'd planned. Diane had managed to kill herself in prison while awaiting trial, something Melody knew she should've been upset about, but couldn't bring herself to be.

"I expect you to tell me what you need from me until they're home. If you need me to bring your food down here, I will. If you need me to leave you alone, I will. If you need a quick fuck, I'm your girl. Just don't block me out. You have a tendency to get a bit single-minded when you're working, and because these are your friends, I'm worried you won't take care of yourself. You need to stand up and walk around every hour. Don't forget to take off your prosthetic every now and then. In fact, I'll send Akilah down to remind you, and you two can clean and massage your stumps together, and—"

Tex cut Melody off by pulling her face to his and kissing the stuffing out of her. "Thank you for taking care of me. If I get too absorbed, I give you permission to get in my face."

"All I'm asking is, don't be a stranger. You know

Baby misses you when you get too deep into your work."

Tex smiled. "God forbid the dog misses me."

Melody smiled back. "Okay, I miss you too."

Tex ran his hand down Melody's chest, not missing how her nipples tightened at his touch. "I've got a while before the mission starts...have any ideas on how we can pass the time?"

Melody smirked and pushed into Tex's hand, encouraging him to continue his caresses. "I might have an idea or two. I'm not sure we've tested this particular chair before, have we? Think it can hold up if I take you right here?"

"Now's a great time to try it and see."

COMMANDER HURT STUDIED the orders from the President. He wasn't happy about the mission. He hated having to send his SEALs into an unknown situation. Oh, it happened a lot, but this time the situation wasn't just unknown, it was unstable, full of hate, and they were being set up to fail. Trying to find an American woman, dressed in a burka, in the middle of a refugee camp, filled with other women wearing similar outfits, would be next to impossible. Not to mention the disease and unsanitary conditions that were running rampant in the crowded, filthy, treacherous camp.

Four hundred thousand people in a camp in the middle of the hot desert—scared, worried and unstable—was a recipe for disaster. The only redeeming factor for the mission was that it was under JSOC command. Joint Special Operations Command was in charge and the mission would involve another SEAL team based out of Norfolk, an Army Ranger team, the Army Night Stalkers would pilot the helos, and, if needed, a Delta Force unit was on standby.

The President's constituents weren't happy that Penelope had been kidnapped and was being used as a pawn in ISIS's deadly game. The world had seen way too many videos of the torture the terrorists put their captives through, and it would be a huge public relations nightmare if Sergeant Penelope Turner ended up in one of those gruesome videos. She was now the country's sister, daughter, friend, and the face of this horrible new war.

Her family, most especially her brother, had been pushing hard and gaining the support of many influential politicians to go in and find his sister. Homeland Security had received enough credible reports that the woman was being held in the refugee camp for the President to authorize a rescue attempt.

"Are you all right, Patrick?"

He turned and held out his arm and sighed when his wife, Julie, snuggled into his side. He felt one arm snake around his belly and the other around his back.

"Yeah, I'm okay."

"I don't think you are. Is it my SEALs?"

Patrick smiled at Julie's terminology. She knew he commanded several different SEAL teams, but she always referred to Cookie and the rest of the men as "hers" since they'd rescued her from Mexico.

Over the years, she'd remained friendly with all their women. She helped Jessyka match up some of the teenagers in the after-school program with prom dresses. Summer had gotten Julie's store included in her company's annual donation campaign, and Julie and Cheyenne emailed each other all the time.

Patrick knew her relationship with Fiona took a lot of hard work to cultivate. She didn't push, but went out of her way to make sure Fiona knew she was thinking about her and to try to be friendly. Just as Patrick had predicted, Julie and his men's wives weren't best friends, but they did seem to enjoy each other's company when they met up at company get-togethers.

"You know I can't say much, but yes, your SEALs are leaving for a mission in the morning."

"Should I call Fiona and see how she's doing? Maybe we should invite her over, make sure she's okay. I can take some time off from the store. My employees know what they're doing, and now that I've hired some of the teenagers to take my place at the front, I'm really just in the way when I'm there anyway. Maybe I can—"

Patrick leaned down and kissed Julie quiet. When he felt her melt into him, he pulled away. "I'm sure she'd love to hear from you, sweetheart." When Julie nodded and moved her hand lower until it brushed against his quickly hardening shaft, Patrick smiled down at her.

"Come to bed. I can tell you're tense, let me help you lose some of that tension."

"I love you, Julie. I'll be there in a little bit."

"Okay, but don't take too long or I'll have to take matters into my own hands," Julie teased.

Patrick leaned down, kissed his wife once again and set her away from him. "Feel free to get yourself off, but know that when I get there I'll be making you come at least twice before I get my turn…so you might want to pace yourself."

Julie blushed and backed away, smiling. Patrick watched until she disappeared around the door to his home office, and he turned his attention back to the file in front of him, distracted with thoughts of his wife now, but still concerned for his men.

The commander in him hoped like hell it wouldn't be a futile mission that would end in the deaths of one, or more, of the finest men he'd ever known. He certainly didn't want Sergeant. Turner to die at the hands of terrorists, but he especially didn't want to have to tell any of the women and children of his own men, who he'd come to know and respect, that their husband, or father, wouldn't be coming home ever again.

Finally, with a small sigh and a quick prayer, Patrick locked the file back into the small office safe and tried to shake off the uneasy feeling he'd had since first seeing the orders. He had a wife to satisfy. He'd take the time to concentrate on her, and on how much he loved her, before having to delve back into the dangerous world of the SEALs the next day. He needed Julie's brand of relaxation.

# Chapter Four

WOLF GAZED AROUND the tent at his men. It'd been a tough forty-eight hours. They'd flown to the Middle East, done a HALO—a high-altitude, low-opening parachute drop—to get into Turkey undetected. They'd thought about jumping into Syria instead, but finally decided they'd be stealthier if they came in from the Turkish side and tried to blend in with the other aid workers.

They'd made the landing without issue and headed to the refugee camp near the city of Cizre, Turkey. It was exactly as described by their commander and as the intelligence had reported. It smelled horrible, and sickness was rampant all around them. They hadn't even been there that long and they'd already witnessed two mothers crying hysterically while clutching their dead babies. None of the team knew what the infants had died from, but ultimately it didn't matter. Dehydration, disease, starvation...seeing the dead babies reminded them all a bit too much of their families back home.

"What's the plan for today?" Abe asked.

Wolf laid out the aerial photographs of the camp they'd received back in California. "The best way to do this is a grid search, but we all know, if Turner is here, they're moving her around. They probably don't spend the night in the same spot twice or at least more than a couple nights. So a grid search won't do us much good. We'll have to cover a lot of ground in this shithole every day so we'll need to break up into teams. We can cover more area in groups of two than if we patrolled together, and we'll blend in better. But remember, that's how we think ISIS got ahold of Turner and the others...they were separated from the rest of the patrol. And we all know ISIS would love to get ahold of a SEAL, so stay on your toes. Everyone has their radios, right?"

The men all nodded, so Wolf continued, "Okay, Benny, you're with me. Dude and Abe, you're together, and Cookie and Mozart. Benny and I will take the left side." Wolf pointed out the area on his map. "Dude, you and Abe take the middle, and Cookie and Mozart, you're on the right. Cover as much ground as you can, be observant, but not obvious. Turner is small, five foot two. She's got light-blonde hair, so if it's not completely covered up, she'll stick out like a sore thumb around here."

"What if they *do* have it covered up?" Benny asked seriously.

"Then we're fucked," Wolf said succinctly. "If she's covered from head to toe in robes, or if they've got her in a burka, there's no way we'll be able to spot her. But be on the guard for groups of young men looking suspicious. Hell, look around. Most people are concerned about food and water; if you see any group of men looking fit and healthy, that's suspicious. Also, the men are armed. Perhaps blatantly so. Abe, got any other ideas?"

"The American and British troops in the area haven't been much help. Intel from Commander Hurt says no one really knows where the soldiers were when they were taken and there's been no sign of Sergeant Turner since she and the others were snatched," Abe said. He took a deep breath, then continued, "I think we should take the first day or so to get the lay of the land, walk around and see what we can find out. But if we don't immediately spot her, we should use the interpreters. Fall into the role of aid worker more deeply. See if we can't find out from the refugees who they're afraid of. The Syrians aren't stupid. If they aren't in ISIS, they probably know who they should keep away from. Since none of us know Turkish, we'll have to rely on the interpreters."

Wolf nodded. "Good. Whatever you do, don't start a war in the middle of the camp. Our objective is to identify the target, and steal her away. We don't want to start a firefight, otherwise a lot of innocent people could die, and the last thing either government wants is an incident. It's a snatch-and-grab if we can swing it."

"What if she's injured or if she's been abused?" Dude asked calmly. Although they could all see he was anything but calm.

"We take her however we can. If she freaks out, knock her out. If she can't walk, carry her. If she's scared of us, do what you can to reassure her. Whatever you do, get the fuck out as soon as you can. Got it?"

All five men nodded at Wolf. They'd all thought the mission was going to be hell, but now that they were here in person, and could see the living conditions of everyone around them, they were sure of it.

"We'll set out first thing in the morning. I know none of us have gotten much sleep in the last two days. Sleep tonight and hopefully we'll be out of this dump sooner rather than later."

The men settled down on their sleeping mats, each lost in their own thoughts about their wife, kids, and what they might find, *if* they find, America's Darling, Sergeant Penelope Turner.

THE NEXT MORNING the men were up and ready before the sun came up. They headed out in pairs, ready for anything. Meeting back at the tent they'd been assigned by the aid workers that night, each pair of men reported what they'd observed.

"The west side of the camp looks to be the older side. The shelters are more established and the people there seem more settled," Cookie told the group. I think it looks promising for the general area where Turner could be held. There wasn't a lot of love for us as we walked around and when Mozart asked some of the other aid workers about that area, they said they rarely ventured too far into that side because they didn't feel safe."

Wolf nodded. "Makes sense. We were on the other side and there were a lot of women and children over there."

"That could be a good place to hide her," Dude commented, trying to play Devil's Advocate.

"Yeah, but most of the men we saw were either very old or very young. It doesn't seem to be a hotbed of ISIS activity. At least not at first glance," Wolf cautioned.

"So it sounds like we can stick to the west and middle tomorrow then," Abe said. "The center of camp seems to be a mix of families, single people, and kids."

"Did anyone see anything that screamed 'terrorist camp' or did you get a glimpse of anyone that could be our target?" Wolf asked the group.

The men all shook their heads. "Not really. The robes and veils make this op almost impossible," Cookie grumbled.

"We have to find her. I can't bear to think of her in this shithole at the hands of those assholes," Dude said, running a hand through his hair.

"We'll do our best." Wolf's words were heartfelt, but they all knew they weren't enough. They had to find this woman. "We'll head out first thing in the morning. After tomorrow, we'll take shifts and walk through the nights as well."

"I'll take the first night shift," Dude volunteered. Wolf looked at his friend critically, knowing Dude wasn't sleeping well because he was worried about Cheyenne and the pregnancy. He nodded. "That's fine. I'll work it with you to start."

SERGEANT PENELOPE TURNER was pissed off. She figured she probably should be scared or freaked-out, but honestly? She was just plain angry. As far as being kidnapped and held by terrorists went, she'd been lucky. They'd beaten the shit out of her the first couple of days they'd had her, but after the first video had gone viral, they'd realized she was more valuable as a propaganda tool than anything else.

They'd asked if she was a virgin, and Penelope had thought long and hard about which would be the best way to answer, and finally she'd admitted that she was not. She hadn't been raped...yet, but figured the men were saving that as a torture technique for later if they needed it.

She'd been forced to read long soliloquies about ISIS's complaints with the West and America, and honestly Penelope had no heartburn over reading whatever they wanted her to. She'd read *War and Peace* if they asked her to. It wasn't as if she really believed what she was reading, and figured America in general would probably understand she was being forced to say the things she was.

But she *did* care about her fellow soldiers. She hadn't seen her friends since they'd been kidnapped. Penelope had no idea how long she'd been in the company of the terrorist group, but thought it'd been around two months.

Thomas Black and Henry White were hilarious. Thomas was from Maine and had red hair and freckles. He frequently joked that he was a down-home "ginger from the north." Henry was from Mississippi and had the darkest skin Penelope had ever seen on anyone before. They'd been teased by the other soldiers, since Thomas's last name was Black and Henry's last name was White, and they were complete opposites of their names. But the men were close friends. They'd bonded the first time they met and had done everything together since they'd arrived in the Middle East. They made an oddly striking pair, but friendship knew no color in the Army. The third man, Robert Wilson, Penelope didn't know very well, but he'd been friendly enough to her and she worried about him just as much as Thomas and Henry.

She figured they were all probably dead, and that pissed her off even more. These ISIS assholes didn't have the right to kill anyone, not when *they* were the ones terrorizing the poor people all around them and kidnapping innocent soldiers like her and her friends who were just trying to help the refugees.

Penelope had volunteered to come over to Turkey to help people and provide some much needed help at the camps. Her Reserve unit, stationed out of Fort Hood, Texas, had sent a company of soldiers, around one hundred and twenty people, to help provide security at the camp. From the second they'd landed, it'd been obvious the major in charge of the troops at the refugee camp wasn't a very good leader. Even though the captains and lieutenants tried to explain how dangerous the security patrols could be, they were still ordered to scout in small groups which could be easily overwhelmed.

She, White, Black, and Wilson had been ordered to patrol the west side of the camp one day, and when she'd protested, claiming it was too dangerous to send them in alone, she'd been reprimanded publically and told to suck it up.

She knew it was because she was a woman and actually had the guts to speak up. If she'd been a man, maybe they would've taken her more seriously. But they'd been sent off with the proverbial pat on the head and look what had happened. Penelope was fucking right and she'd been stuck in this hellhole for who knew how long.

Penelope had wanted to escape long before now, but the assholes who'd kidnapped her weren't actually as idiotic as she'd hoped, or as they'd seemed at first. They moved her almost every night to a different tent. They only allowed her outside whatever tent they were keeping her in if she was covered from head to toe in the flowing robes and garments the women in the region wore.

Penelope knew her blonde hair would give her away if she dared take off the covering. She'd thought about it more than once, simply whipping the material off her head and running screaming through the camp, but she'd seen how the men around her were. She'd either be shot dead immediately, or she'd suffer horribly and wish she was dead long before they were done with her. So far, she hadn't been raped, tortured, burned alive, or had her head cut off, and she took all of that as a win.

So she was in limbo. Waiting for something to happen.

One good thing—Penelope always tried to find good in every situation—was that the everyday thugs in the camp were scared of ISIS. She didn't have to worry about them on top of everything else she worried about.

So she waited. Day in and day out, pretending to be meek and scared, while silently seething inside and on the lookout for something, anything, that would get her out of there. If she made it home, and could hug her brother, she'd never step foot outside Texas again.

The sounds of the camp faded around her. They never really quieted all the way, but they did settle down as night fell. Penelope figured most people were scared to walk around when the sun dipped below the horizon, as well they should be.

The door to the tent opened and Penelope quickly looked down, trying not to make eye contact with whoever it was who'd entered her tent. She'd learned the hard way that looking one of the terrorists in the eye only set them off.

"Up," he grunted.

Some of her guards spoke excellent English, while others knew only the basic words. She thought about trying to send some message on the videos she was forced to record, but knew there were too many people around her and involved with ISIS who knew English. The video would never make it out and they'd probably kill her for daring to defy them. It made more sense to bide her time and pray she'd get the chance to escape or that someone would come to free her.

She stood up at the guard's request. He shoved the robe at her that she'd been forced to wear every time they moved. "Put it on."

Penelope sighed. Looked like it was moving time. She hated the robe with a passion. It was hot, and stunk like pee, sweat, and who knew what the hell else. But shit, *she* stunk; she couldn't really ask for a shower in the middle of the desert.

Moving tents meant uncertainty. She'd been at the same tent now for three nights, an eternity in her world. Penelope held her breath and slipped the foul garment over her head, doing what her captor demanded, and hoped like hell this would end…preferably sooner rather than later, and preferably with her going home, rather than with her head rolling around on the sand after being chopped off.

# Chapter Five

*It's been two months since American Penelope Turner was kidnapped by ISIS operatives. She was participating in a humanitarian mission at the Cizre, Turkey, refugee camp. Thousands of Syrians have been streaming over the border, on the run from the multiple terrorist groups and the ethnic cleansing in Syria.*

*Sergeant Turner was snatched while on a routine patrol of the camp, along with three other men. You might remember Thomas Black and Henry White were beheaded and nailed to a cross, and Robert Wilson was set on fire while still alive.*

*There have been conflicting reports of where Turner might be held captive, but sources say the U.S. Government has been looking into rescue attempts. All efforts to get more information on this possibility have been ignored or deflected by the White House Director of Communication.*

*Penelope's brother has been leading the charge to get troops to head into Syria to look for his sister.*

*There is an online petition with over one hundred thousand signatures gathered so far, addressed to the President, to try to urge him to do something to rescue his sister.*

*The video of Cade Turner being interviewed by our affiliate station in San Antonio, Texas, has gone viral. His impassioned statement of, "Fine, don't negotiate with the terrorists, just go in and get her the BLEEP out," has resonated with Americans throughout the country. There have been T-shirts, bumper stickers, and even posters made with Cade's statement. America wants Penelope Turner home.*

*There has been no video of Sergeant Turner since the last one released two weeks ago.*

CAROLINE CUDDLED JOHN in her lap as Brinique and Davisa tried to entertain Sara. Watching the five and six-year-old interact with two-year-old Sara was endearing and entertaining as hell.

"How you holding up, Jess?" Alabama asked her friend.

"I'm okay, thanks. Caroline, I appreciate you letting me stay with you for a few days."

"No problem. You know I love having you guys here."

"Do you think they're all right?"

They all knew who Jess was asking about.

"Yes. I'm sure they're fine," Caroline tried to soothe. "It's just...Kason was more worried than usual about this mission."

"Christopher was too. Should we be concerned?" Alabama's voice was muted so her daughters couldn't hear her.

Caroline wanted to tell her friends what she suspected, but kept it to herself, as she knew Matthew would want her to. "No. Our men are professionals. They know what they're doing. They'd be irritated if we sat at home and cried all the time about them. They've been gone before and we were fine. This is the same thing."

The other two women nodded, but didn't look appeased.

"We should get out of the house and have some fun today," Caroline told them decidedly.

"I need to go and check on the bar. Fiona's working today. We could go and visit her."

"Perfect!" Caroline exclaimed. "I'm so happy for you. You totally deserved to be named manager after Mr. Davis retired."

"He said if it worked out, he'd consider selling it to me as well," Jessyka told her friends.

"Oh my God. That's awesome!" Alabama got up and hugged Jess. "When were you going to tell us? Does anyone else know?"

"Well, Fiona knows. She would have to, since she's

the assistant manager."

"Good for you. Let's see if we can't get these kids packed up in under an hour. Lord, I had no idea it took so long to get out of the house with kids in tow," Alabama mock grumbled.

"It takes even longer when they're *this* age," Jess said, motioning to her two. "I've gotten to the point where whatever Sara wants to wear, I let her. It's easier than arguing with her about it. And believe me, you never win when arguing with a two-year-old!"

They all laughed and stood to get ready to go.

An hour later the group made their way inside *Aces*. It was early enough that most of the patrons were eating a late lunch and the alcohol hadn't started to flow yet. Caroline knew Alabama wouldn't bring her daughters into the bar if there was the slightest chance anything inappropriate would be going on.

"Feeeeeeeee!" Sara screeched, toddling her way into the room and looking for her favorite babysitter.

Fiona stuck her head out the office door down the long hall and laughed as Sara waddled her way to her with her arms outstretched. She snatched the little girl up before she could fall and swung her around in a circle before sitting her on her hip. "Hey, pretty girl. What brings you and your mommy and brother here today?"

"Twip!"

"A trip, huh?" Fiona laughed and looked at Jess,

who was limping down the hall toward her.

"Caroline decided we all needed some air, so here we are."

"Well, I'm glad to see you. I need a break too. My eyes are crossing from looking at numbers."

"I told them about the bar," Jess told her friend.

"Good. It's about time. They were happy for you, weren't they?"

Jess smiled. "Yeah. Come on, take a break with us. I'm sure Alabama has Brinique and Davisa settled in with some ice cream and I'm afraid if I leave John with Caroline for too long, she'll steal him from me."

The two women laughed at Jess's long-standing joke as they went back into the main room and joined their friends.

After sitting for a while and laughing at the antics of the kids, and commenting on how good of a baby John was, Jess excused herself and headed for the bathroom.

Caroline handed John off to Fiona and headed after Jess, wanting to make sure she was all right. She found her kneeling in front of one the toilets, having thrown up the delicious snack they'd just eaten.

"Are you all right?"

"Shit, Caroline. I'm so screwed."

"What? Are you sick? Do you need to go to the doctor?"

Jess snorted and leaned back on her heels and wiped

her mouth. "No, I'm not sick in the sense you're talking about."

Caroline seemed to suddenly understand. "Oh lord. You're pregnant again?"

"Yeah, I think so. I haven't taken a test or anything, and I only started feeling nauseous yesterday and today. But I recognize the signs. I feel like I'm the only person on the planet who gets afternoon sickness instead of morning sickness."

Caroline giggled, she couldn't help it, and laughed outright when Jess glared up at her from her crouching position on the floor. "Come on, let me help you up." Caroline reached out a hand, relieved when Jess accepted it. Between the two of them, they got Jess off the floor. "I've never met anyone as fertile as you and Kason."

"I know, it's ridiculous. We said we were gonna wait and put a bit more time between John and a new brother or sister."

"What happened?"

Jess gave Caroline an evil look and held it even as Caroline laughed at her. "Oh, yeah. Our men are horny devils, aren't they?"

"He promised to use condoms because he knows birth control pills make me feel bloated and they wreak havoc with my moods," Jess grumbled. "But then you had to be all noble and offer to babysit John and Sara for an entire weekend. We were really careful the first night, but as the weekend went on, we got more and more lazy…and here I am."

Caroline gave Jessyka a big hug. "Well, congrats, woman."

"I still need to take a test to find out for certain, but I'm pretty sure. I recognize this feeling." Jess put a hand on her still-rounded stomach from the baby weight she hadn't been able to lose after having John. "As much as it freaks me out, I have to say I'm pretty happy. I'd give Kason a million babies if I could."

"A million is a bit much, you dork. If you want to set up a doctor's appointment, you know I'll either babysit for you or hold your hand when you go."

"I wish Kason was here."

"I know you do. But you'll get through this just fine. It's what we Navy SEAL wives do. We keep on keepin' on while our men are off saving the world. Just think about how you want to let Kason know when he gets home that he's going to be a father…again."

Jess stood up, washed her hands and swished some water around her mouth. "You're right. We're strong, capable women who don't need a man to be by our side all the time."

"Damn straight. You don't think I'll be able to keep this from the others, do you?"

Jess smiled at Caroline. "You mean you haven't already mind-melded with them to let them know? I'm disappointed in you."

"Hey, I can keep a secret."

"Uh-huh."

"Seriously."

Jess smiled at her friend. "Caroline, I don't care if you tell them. Tell the world. I'm so happy with my life right now, it almost seems unfair to everyone else."

Caroline smiled at Jess. "I'll try to control myself and let you tell the others, but you better start with Alabama and Fiona, who are waiting out at the table for us."

They joined arms and headed out to the bar to tell their friends there'd be another little Sawyer arriving in about seven months.

# Chapter Six

THE SEALS EXASPERATED sighs demonstrated their annoyance with the situation. They'd been at the godforsaken refugee camp for seven days now and hadn't had one glimpse of Penelope Turner or anyone who could possibly be her. Of course, trying to find anyone in the huge tent city was like trying to find a needle in a haystack. They'd uncovered a lot of crooked and criminal shit, but had to ignore it all and focus on their mission.

Wolf knew the long frustrating search was taking its toll on the team. Dude wanted to hurry up and find Penelope not only so they could get her out of the situation, but also so he could get back to Cheyenne. They hadn't had any updates from home, and they were all hoping she hadn't gone into premature labor and had his daughter yet.

Abe was wondering how Brinique and Davisa were doing, and worried about Alabama taking on too much. Benny was in much the same frame of mind and was worrying about Jessyka overdoing things with their two young kids and trying to keep *Aces* up and running.

They all were completely focused on the mission, but couldn't help but worry about their women and children back home.

And in the forefront of all their minds was Penelope Turner. The refugee camp was hell on earth. It was male-dominated, dirty, miserably hot, and the threat of violence hung over the camp like a bomb that was slowly ticking down, every second bringing it closer to detonation. It was obvious all hell could break loose at any moment. It was as if everyone was holding their breath, but they knew they couldn't hold it forever. The thought of Penelope or any vulnerable woman being in the middle of his hellhole, turned all their stomachs.

There were what Wolf called "roving gangs" prowling the camp, especially at night. They were looking for the vulnerable and the weak. The gangs would steal what little food they could find, and if they were in the mood, would rape any female they came across. No one was safe, from the littlest girls to the oldest grandmothers.

The team had no idea if Penelope was safe or if she was suffering the same fate as many of the other females in the camp. There had been no word of another video surfacing, so it was all speculation as to whether she was still alive or even at the camp at all.

Two days ago, another SEAL team had arrived to join in the search for the missing sergeant, and Wolf was damn glad. They could use all the help they could get. The other team was based out of Virginia and had been recommended by Tex to join the mission. Wolf's team had worked with them once before and knew they were extremely competent. Wolf didn't know all the members on the team personally, but was impressed with what he'd seen in the past and thus far out in the desert.

The teams had split up further and combed the refugee camp looking for Penelope. The place was huge, and their job was made tougher because of the burka most of the women wore. Wolf knew many of the women now wore the head-to-toe coverings to try to protect themselves from the men stalking the camp for victims rather than for any religious ideology.

They were on the lookout for a group of men with a lone woman, who would most likely be covered from head to toe in a robe, and she'd be short, at least compared to them. That was about all they had. It would be unusual for a single woman to be with a group of men, as in the Muslim culture, the men tended to hang out with other men and the women banded together as well. The women would do chores around their chosen tent, while the men would gather, talk, and try to find food for their families or groups.

One of the SEALs on the other team, Rocco, spoke

Turkish, thank God. Today's plan was to see what information they could glean from some of the men they'd befriended in their guise as aid workers. Wolf knew most of the groups of Syrians they'd made contact with had a pretty good idea they weren't who they said they were, but so far, their luck had held and they hadn't had any trouble. But they all knew that luck would probably run out sooner rather than later.

If ISIS had any idea there were two groups of elite Navy SEALs in the camp looking for them and Penelope, they'd most likely either kill her and run, or take her with them when they left and probably kill her later, in a very horrific and public way in retaliation. For the moment, the terrorists were feeling safe in the anonymity of the huge refugee camp.

Both SEAL teams knew their time was running out to find Penelope and bring her home alive.

Ace and Gumby, two of the men from the Virginia team, and Cookie and Dude were currently out searching the camp. They'd taken the night shift. The groups had night-vision goggles, but they'd be very obvious if they wore them around the camp, so they'd decided not to use them. But the time was quickly coming where they were going to be needed. They hadn't made any headway thus far and all of the men were becoming frustrated with their lack of success.

The groups radioed back to the others their locations and if they found anything suspicious. One of the men at the tent they'd started calling the Command Tent, or CT, would take notes and mark on a large aerial photo what regions of the camp had been searched and what areas the guys deemed to have suspicious activity and should be rechecked, either another night, or the next day when there was light.

The radio crackled. Abe and a Vietnamese man called Ho Chi Minh, from the other SEAL team, were manning the radios while the other men got some much-needed sleep.

"Rover one to CT." Gumby's voice was quiet and toneless. It was the tone they all used when talking on the radios so as not to bring attention to themselves. The thugs in the camp would kill to get their hands on a high-tech set of radios such as the teams had.

"This is CT. Go ahead."

"Found a ripped piece of pink cloth at coordinates, LG3777633131."

"The same kind as before?" Ho Chi Mien asked.

"Roger."

Abe got up and shook Wolf awake. This was the second piece of pink cloth the teams had found, and there was no way it was a coincidence. First of all, there wasn't a lot of material around that was pink, and second, it was highly unlikely there would be random scraps of pink material floating around the refugee camp. It had to be a fucking clue. They were running on empty and any kind of anomaly, no matter how small, was cause for celebration and worth a second look.

"Wolf," Abe said softly, not touching the man, letting his voice wake him up. "Gumby found a clue."

"I'm up. What is it?" Wolf asked, rolling to his feet, immediately awake. The ability to be asleep one second and completely awake the next was a life-saving skill they'd all gained over the years on the team. And while it might fade when they were home for a while, they could all pick it up without missing a beat while on a mission.

"Pink cloth." Abe didn't have to say anything else.

"Coordinates?"

The men walked over to the table where Ho Chi Mien was marking Gumby's find on the map.

"Looks like it's in the same general area as the other one."

Abe looked at Wolf. "She's fucking leaving us breadcrumbs."

"Don't get your hopes up, it might not be her," Wolf warned, although it was obvious he was more than pleased with the development.

"Yeah, maybe not. But it's more than we had an hour ago."

Wolf nodded and studied the map.

"Your men are meeting up with Gumby and Ace. They'll see what else they can find at the location," Ho Chi Mien stated softly.

Wolf nodded. "Good. Anything is better than what we've got so far at this point. We'll send in the teams tomorrow to search in the daylight. I know Rocco was up late tonight talking with some men, but we need him to go out there and see what the people around the area know."

"No problem," Ho Chi Mien stated immediately. "This has become personal."

"For us too," Abe agreed.

"All we can think of is our women back home," the Asian man continued. "What if this was our girlfriend, or daughter, or sister? I can't blame her brother for putting up as big of a raucous as he has."

"What did we miss?" Wolf asked, obviously not knowing what Ho Chi Mien was talking about in regards to the missing soldier's brother.

"Last I heard, there was an online petition to the President with over two hundred thousand signatures, to go in and do something to rescue her."

Wolf chuckled flatly. "Well, here we are. Doing something."

"Yeah. The guy's been on every news channel giving interviews and telling the world about his sister. They seem to be really close; it's irritating that we can't find her for him."

Abe shook his head at the other SEAL's words. Irritating. Yeah, that about summed it up. "Okay, so let's say this *is* our target. We're still no closer to finding her than we were before."

"Yeah, but now we know what we're looking for, at least somewhat. We know she's leaving clues, and we can try to see if there's a pattern. I'd bet everything I own, these guys are moving her around in fucking circles, using the same hidey-holes. If we can find enough clues to sense their pattern, we can find the missing sergeant," Wolf told his friend and teammate.

Abe nodded. "It's a long shot, but it's all we've got right now."

PENELOPE SIGHED IN frustration. She was hot, tired, and bored. It felt somewhat messed up to say she was bored, but she was. She did nothing all day. She'd started trying to keep her strength up by doing pushups and sit-ups during the day, but she knew she was weakening, and it both irritated and scared her. Without her strength, the ability to escape at a moment's notice was lessened immensely.

Her captors would usually bring her something to eat in the morning, a stale crust of bread, or some sort of mystery-meat stew, and while she wanted to refuse it, she knew she couldn't. The water was disgusting, but again, she needed the liquid. She was on the verge of dehydration as it was, refusing to drink what they brought would be tantamount to suicide.

Her captors were ramping up to something, but Penelope didn't know what. She had no idea if anyone was looking for her, but knowing her brother as she did, she hoped someone was. Just as she'd do for him, Cade wouldn't stop until she was found, dead or alive.

They were extremely close. They weren't too far apart in age and Penelope could remember tagging along after Cade when they were kids…and he'd let her. They even played games together when they were young, just the two of them. One of the games she remembered most vividly was a game they called, "War." There was a field near their house and they'd go hide in the bushes, lying on their bellies and pretending there were bad guys out in the field looking for them. Cade hadn't seemed to care she was a girl, or his younger sister.

As they got older, the games stopped, but Cade's support and love for her never ceased. He was the reason she'd made it as far in the fire service as she had. He was the reason her fellow firefighters supported and trusted her to have their backs. It was Cade's unending and unflagging encouragement she'd received in the past that made her continue to hold on in the hellacious situation she currently found herself in, and the reason she knew he was doing what he could to find her.

So she'd started trying to leave parts of herself behind any chance she could get. Penelope had taken off her panties, they were beyond disgusting at this point anyway, and ripped the seams out. Once upon a time they were her favorite pair. Stupid to bring such a girly pair of underwear on an Army mission in the first place, but she'd always tried to keep her feminine side alive and well, even if it was under her uniform. She might work in a male-dominated profession—well, two of them—but she'd be damned if she lost her femininity altogether. She'd hidden the material under the robes her captors were constantly making her wear, and since, so far, they hadn't had any interest in raping her, the material had gone unnoticed.

Penelope had been leaving little pieces behind, like breadcrumbs. She'd always loved the fairytale Hansel and Gretel growing up. She only hoped they weren't being swept away as she left them, as had happened in the story.

She had no idea who might be looking for her, if anyone, but she hoped with all her heart they were smart and observant. All the places she'd been taken looked the same to her, but it was after she'd been leaving the pieces of cloth for a while, and had been moved again, that she noticed one of her breadcrumbs that she'd left in the past.

The bastards were using the same tents to hold her in. Moving her all the time, yes, but to the same tents over and over again. It gave her hope someone would notice and find her. She only had to wait. But Penelope had no idea how much time she had and hoped it wouldn't run out before someone cottoned on to the trail she was leaving.

"Up. Come."

The words were loud and heavily accented. Penelope jumped a foot. Dammit, she'd been so far inside her head, she hadn't heard the man enter her tent. That shit would get her killed. She stood up and took the robe the man shoved at her. She put it on quickly and winced as the man grabbed her arm and he led her outside.

He force-marched her toward a group of men who were talking excitedly and seemed almost giddy with anticipation. Oh shit, was this it? Was it her time to die? Were they taking her to chop off her head? Death didn't scare her, but knowing they'd record it and show it to the world—and her brother—scared the shit out of her. She didn't want Cade's last glimpse of her to be her head rolling off her neck and onto the ground.

No one said anything as they surrounded her, and the entire group meandered through the refugee camp. Penelope tried to keep track of where they were and where they were headed, but it was impossible. The group finally stopped in front of a large truck and Penelope was shoved into the back and the men all clambered in behind her.

The truck was a deuce and a half…a large truck that looked like it had an eighteen-wheeler type of cab, and a huge sorta pickup type of bed. The back was covered with a large tarp, not unlike what the tents were made out of, and there were two benches. It looked like a military vehicle that had been jerry-rigged to hold a large amount of people. Men were sitting along the benches, and there was a blindfolded man wearing some sort of uniform, arms bound behind his back, kneeling in the back of the truck against the cab.

There were six men already in the truck when their little group climbed aboard, each of the six were holding AK-47 assault rifles. No one spoke to her, but they did talk with each other. Penelope had no idea what was being said, but she had a very bad feeling about what was about to happen.

She looked at the blindfolded man and hoped like hell they'd both make it out alive.

# Chapter Seven

*Another video of kidnapped American Penelope Turner has surfaced. ISIS posted it on their webpage sometime last night. In the video, an Australian soldier is shown being led to an unknown location and being forced to lean over a large boulder. He was blindfolded and had his arms tied behind his back.*

*The Australian government says the man is Thomas Bauer, a lieutenant in the Australian Army. He was apparently taken two days ago from the same refugee camp where Turner and the other murdered Americans had been working. As a result of the multiple kidnappings and murders, most countries have ceased humanitarian efforts in the region and are quietly pulling out their troops.*

*In the video, Bauer isn't given a chance to say anything, but is beheaded after a man in a mask reads a manifesto of some sort in Arabic. Immediately after the murder, a woman, believed to be Penelope Turner, reads a long letter, presumably written by the terrorists, denouncing Australia's partnership with the West, specifically the United States, and warning there will be more kidnappings and beheadings to come, all in the name of Allah.*

*Several Islamic religious groups in the Washington DC area have converged in a peaceful march to show the world, and the U.S., that their religion does not preach hate and to show they are not in support of what ISIS is doing in the name of their God.*

*Cade Turner, the brother of the kidnapped Sergeant Turner, will be on an hour-long special broadcast tonight to discuss the latest development and what it might mean for his sister.*

CAROLINE SAT TRANSFIXED, staring at the television. She'd been trying to follow the case of the missing American soldier, but every time she saw or heard anything, it made her stomach hurt. She knew, deep in her gut, the guys were over there trying to find her. She felt horrible for the woman's brother. He was on all the talk and news shows. She hoped like hell Matthew and the team could bring her home, but Caroline was selfish. She wanted her man home, where he was safe.

She couldn't talk about what she thought was going on or where she figured the men were with the other women, so as not to worry them, and it was eating her up inside.

The phone rang, scaring the bejeezus out of Caroline. She laughed a bit and muted the television and answered.

"Hello?"

"Hey, Caroline. It's Melody. How are you?"

"Melody! It's great to hear from you! I'm good. How are you and Tex and Akilah?"

"We're good. Tex actually found a therapist who speaks Arabic. I really think it's helped her."

"That's awesome. I totally need to take a trip out there to see you all. Hell, without any drama the last two years, I've missed talking to Tex."

"I'll tell him to call you more often." Melody paused, then asked, "How is everyone holding up? How are *you* holding up?"

"It's tough. I miss Matthew more than ever, and with Cheyenne being about to pop any day now, I know she's more stressed than she's ever been. Of course everyone is trying to hide it, and doing a crap job of it."

Melody laughed lightly. "If it makes you feel any better, Tex has been holed up in the basement with his computers for the last two weeks since they left."

Caroline sighed. "Actually, yeah, that does make me feel a lot better. I know Tex is there and they are…wherever they are…but knowing he's watching over the guys makes me feel better."

"And you."

"What?"

"He's watching over you and the others too."

"And I appreciate that. After everything that's happened to us in the past, it's good."

"What I'm saying is that Tex will know if Cheyenne goes to the hospital, so he can get word to the guys. When that baby starts coming, don't worry about taking the time to call Commander Hurt. Tex will take care of it."

"Thanks. Please tell Tex thanks too."

"You know I will."

"Melody, have you been watching the news?" Caroline knew she was treading on dangerous ground, but since Melody wasn't technically a SEAL wife—Tex was retired, after all—she didn't feel as if she was breaking the unspoken rules as badly as if she'd brought up her concerns with any of her friends there in California. Caroline wasn't a SEAL, so she wasn't under any obligation to keep any of her guesses as to where the men were or what they were doing to herself, but in order to spare her friends, they had enough on their minds, she decided to speak to Melody about it.

"Yeah. Anything specifically?"

"Penelope Turner."

"Ah."

Caroline waited for Melody to say something else.

"That's a sucky situation."

"Do you think they'll find her?"

"Yeah. If anyone can, they can."

And there it was. Additional confirmation that what Caroline had thought was true. She knew Tex most likely wasn't sharing details with Melody, he was as secretive as anyone she'd ever met, but Melody was smart. She could read between the lines just as well as Caroline could. The guys *were* in Turkey. They *were* looking for the missing soldier. And they *were* most likely in a lot of danger. Just the thought of ISIS getting hold of a SEAL made Caroline shudder in horror.

"I'm scared, Melody," she whispered, as if the very words spoken aloud would make something horrible happen.

"Me too. You keep it hidden well though. You're the glue that holds the girls together. They all rely on you, Caroline. You're their rock."

"I know," Caroline whispered. "I don't know if I'm worthy of it though."

"You are. You know how I know?"

"How?"

"Because you're scared out of your mind, but you aren't letting on. You're going to work, you're babysitting, you're going out with them to keep their mind off of their men. You're probably Cheyenne's new breathing coach since Dude isn't there…right?" Melody didn't wait for Caroline to respond. "That's *your* posse, and nothing is going to touch them as long as you're around." It wasn't a question.

"I *am* scared."

"Of course you are. I'd be worried about you if you weren't."

"Matthew is *my* rock. I depend on him. I lean on him. I'm good when he's not here because I know he'll be back and I can let some of my worries and responsibilities slide. He'll pick up the slack. But this time—"

"No, don't even say it."

"But—"

"No. I mean it, Caroline. You can't think that way. Ever. But here's what I know. *You're* the rock. You just think Matthew is because he's your match, but in reality, you are *his* rock. Remember back to when you were kidnapped. Jesus, Caroline, you were beaten, shot and left to die in the freaking ocean. But you didn't. You held on. For Matthew. Don't you think he'd move heaven and earth to come back to you?"

Caroline sobbed once, then ruthlessly controlled it. Melody was right. "You're right."

"Of course I am."

A short laugh escaped Caroline. "When are you coming to visit again?"

"Actually, that's why I called in the first place. Tex

basically ordered me out of the house. I'd like to come visit and bring Akilah, if at all possible."

"Hell yeah. I'd love to see you guys. The basement apartment is always open for you."

"Thanks. I didn't think you'd say no. Tex already got us tickets."

They both laughed. "It'll be good to see you, Mel," Caroline said honestly. "I could use a distraction."

"That's me…one distraction, coming right up."

"Thanks. Send me the details and I'll be sure to be waiting at the airport for you. I'll also tell the girls. Maybe it'll give Cheyenne some incentive to hold that baby inside for a while longer, although I'm not sure Faulkner is gonna make it home in time."

"I don't know either, but you never know, they might get lucky."

# Chapter Eight

HELL, WE MIGHT *just get lucky,* Wolf thought to himself as he and Dude scoured the most likely area where Penelope was being held. After the Australian soldier had been killed, the SEAL teams had doubled their efforts to find any kind of clue Penelope might be leaving behind. The international forces that were at the camp were slowly pulling out, because the danger finally outweighed the benefits of being there. Their exit made the SEALs' existence at the camp shaky. Being the only western-looking soldiers there wasn't a good thing and made them stand out like sore thumbs.

ISIS was still using Penelope as their spokesperson, and it was effective as hell. Wolf knew the news channels all over the world would have no problem showing the petite, fragile-looking woman reading the manifestos the terrorists had written. It was a great way to get the word out to the world and to spread their hate.

The SEALs were *not* happy that she was obviously present at the last beheading, and hated how her voice had quavered while she'd read ISIS's hateful words right after the Australian soldier had been killed. She might be a soldier and trained for combat, but she was also a woman, and every man on the teams wanted to shield her from what she was obviously seeing and going through.

But while she had to be scared out of her mind, she was also holding on. She was smart. It'd taken Bubba, another Virginia SEAL team member, and Mozart two days to find all of her subtle clues. She was anchoring a piece of the pink cloth to the bottom outside edge of the tent she was most likely being held in. She probably reached under the tarp from the inside and secured it so it could be seen from the outside. It wasn't obvious; Bubba was the first to find the small clue, and Mozart wasn't sure at first it was even a clue at all.

But after Mozart found another attached to the back side of a tent not too far from the first, it was as obvious as if she'd stood up and screamed, 'Here I am!'"

It'd taken a week to determine any kind of pattern and to find as many clues as possible, but when all her pink so-called flags had been marked on the map, the pattern was clear. How many nights she was being kept at each tent was unknown and probably varied, but it looked as if they were simply rotating her to the same tents over and over again.

Both teams were on reconnaissance that night. They

had to figure out which tent Sergeant Turner was being held in, and plan the best way to get her out. They would find her tonight, and tomorrow they'd get the fuck out of dodge.

There were five teams of two searching the camp, and two men back at the command tent waiting for information. Wolf and Dude slowly made their way toward their objective. Wolf thought there was a pretty good chance Penelope would be there because, after analyzing the probability and knowing where she'd been, and when, this tent hadn't been used in a couple of days. It was due.

Occasionally tripping over objects left in their path, the men heard snoring, groaning, moaning, and the occasional unmistakable sound of sex as they made their way through the dark passageways of the camp. They'd reached the end of the row of tents they were searching and the light of the morning sunrise was about to peek over the horizon.

The men stopped in their tracks at the sound of English somewhere nearby. They hadn't heard English being spoken by anyone outside their team since they'd arrived at the camp. They stopped to listen. The voice was faint and irritated and they could only hear part of what was being said.

*"Motherfuckers. What's … so goddamn long? I've left … breadcrumbs for a fucking child to find… Are they*

*incompetent or what?"*

The mutterings continued, and Wolf and Dude smiled at each other. They were so thankful to hear what had to be Sergeant Penelope Turner's irritated voice, they didn't even care she'd been disparaging them. Hell, her feisty attitude was a welcome sound. It would hopefully be much easier to rescue her than if she was beaten down and terrified. They'd take a pissed-off soldier, ready to get the hell out, over a hysterical, crying woman any day of the week.

"Rover five to CT." Wolf's voice was low and barely audible as he spoke into his radio.

"This is CT."

"Target located."

"Repeat."

"Target. Fucking. Located," Wolf enunciated again into the radio, not able to keep the enthusiasm out of his voice this time.

"You're cutting out, but did I hear Target located? Confirm." Cookie's voice was also hushed, but Wolf could hear the excitement cutting through his no-nonsense words anyway.

"Affirmative."

"Copy that. Target located and location marked. Will notify other rovers. Out."

Wolf clipped the radio to his belt and motioned to Dude. They slunk back through the dark the way they'd come. They hated to leave Penelope, but they had a rescue to plan, they couldn't go by the seat of their pants on this one. No way would they risk losing her that way.

By this time tomorrow, they'd all be well on their way to the Special Forces base at Yuksekova, about two hundred miles east, and then on their way home. Halle-fucking-lujah.

PENELOPE SAT ON the ground in the newest tent she'd been moved to, drew her knees up in front of her and clasped her hands around them. For what seemed like the millionth time, she pushed her hair out of her face. She'd literally kill someone for a shower. If they were standing between her and fresh, clean water—cold or hot didn't matter at this point—she'd use her bare hands to kill them to get at it. But a shower was so far outside what she could imagine happening, it wasn't even funny.

Her hair felt greasy and nasty and she had several snarls in it that she knew would take a miracle to get out without cutting off all her hair. Her hands were gray with dirt and her fingernails were torn and ragged and had dirt caked under them. She itched, and figured she probably had lice or some other nasty bug infestation. The hair on her legs and under her arms was long and she sometimes felt like a hairy beast. But she was alive.

And she'd stay that way as long as she could and would endure bugs, dirt, and body hair that was way too long for her comfort for as long as it'd take to be rescued.

But it was the thirst that was the hardest thing to endure. The heat of the desert, along with the hot-as-hell tents she'd been holed up in, were finally starting to wear her body down. She wasn't even sweating anymore and the few times she'd broken down, she didn't even have enough extra water in her body for tears to fall from her eyes. Her muscles frequently cramped up from lack of water. Penelope knew her body would continue to slowly shut down if she didn't get more water. She'd been drinking questionable warm water for weeks now. She'd been really sick the first few weeks, but figured her body had acclimated to whatever organisms were swimming in the little water she did get. But it wasn't enough. It was *never* enough.

The night before, when she'd been moved, had been different. She hadn't seen any of the men who'd been in charge of her before, and the men who'd moved her had been way more "handsy" than anyone had been in the past. Penelope didn't think that boded well for her future.

She thought about her brother again. Cade wouldn't allow the government to forget about her, or give up, of that she had no doubt. Even if she was killed over here in the desert, Cade would make sure she was remembered. Hell, he'd probably lobby to get her name added to history books or something. Penelope knew she was tired when she didn't even smile at the thought.

When Cade had decided to be a firefighter, Penelope decided she'd be one too. He hadn't laughed, or tried to talk her out of it, he encouraged and bullied her until she'd made it. When she'd thought about going into the Reserves, again, he'd encouraged her and told her she'd be awesome at whatever she decided to do with her life. Cade made her a better human being and was the one person Penelope longed to see again. As one of her best friends, *he* was who she missed the most.

Penelope knew she wasn't the tallest woman in the world, and that most people underestimated her. She was strong. Well, she *used* to be strong, before she'd been underfed, confined, and not able to work out other than the occasional sit-ups and pushups. She wasn't looking her best at the moment; months with no shower would do that to a person. But she wasn't going to give up. Not until a bullet was entering her brain or a big-ass machete was cutting her head from her shoulders.

She remembered how the Australian soldier hadn't fought or cried. He'd been stoic, almost resigned to the fact he was going to die. Penelope had no idea if she'd be able to be as calm as he was when it was her turn to face death. She'd most likely fight like hell until her captors managed to kill her.

She'd taken up talking to herself, if nothing else, simply to hear the English language. "I'll never complain about someone talking too much again. I'd give anything to have a real conversation with someone. Forget the pigeon-English shit."

Penelope put her head down on her knees and tried to ignore the warmth of the tent she was in. As the sun rose high in the sky, so did the temperature. Because she couldn't sweat, she dreamed about the days when she came out of training or got through with working out, covered in sweat, and tilted up her water bottle to quench her thirst.

One day at a time. She had to make it through one day at a time. Someone would find her. They had to. She was slowly losing her mind.

# Chapter Nine

WOLF, ABE, COOKIE, MOZART, DUDE, BENNY, and the six members of the other SEAL team, Rocco, Gumby, Ace, Ho Chi Mien, Bubba, and Rex, huddled around the map. Wolf explained the extraction plan for the third time, making sure everyone knew exactly where they were supposed to be and when.

The plan was for Rex and his team to cause a distraction near the area where Penelope was being held, but not close enough to cause suspicion. Wolf's team would move in, under the cover of darkness and ensuing chaos. Dude and Cookie would enter through the back of the tent and extract the sergeant. After they extracted her, Wolf and Benny would lead the way and Abe and Mozart would take up the rear.

They'd contacted the JSOC and the plan was for the Night Stalkers, the Army's elite helicopter crew, to swoop in on the other side of the camp and pick them up. They'd fly the two hundred miles east to the Special Forces base at Yuksekova, and there Penelope would be seen by a doctor. They'd all be flown to Ramstein Air Base in Germany, where she could be examined more thoroughly by the base's medical team, and then they'd all head home.

After Wolf's group was safely away with Penelope, the Virginia SEAL team would slip back to their command tent and hike north away from the camp, and be picked up by another Night Stalker team.

The entire operation should take no more than thirty minutes to extract Penelope, two hours to fly to the Special Forces Base, and they should be home within thirty six hours after that.

Of course, they'd all learned that the only sure thing in a mission was that something could go wrong, and the only easy day was yesterday, so they had a Plan B and a Plan C.

The first thing that was most obviously wrong before they even set out to rescue Sergeant Turner was that the batteries in their radios were dying. The hell of it was, they couldn't do anything about it. Batteries died. Period. It wasn't feasible to carry a pocket full of replacement batteries on a mission, and anyway, the ones in the radios were rechargeable. They'd each brought an extra pack, but with the increased usage of the electronics at the camp during their patrols and searches, those had also been exhausted.

Without any electricity they hadn't been able to

charge them back up, and even if they'd known they'd be out of pocket for as long as they had been, there wouldn't have been anything they could've done to prevent the batteries from dying. Rex had given Dude one of their radios, since their batteries were a week newer than Wolf's team, but they were seriously screwed if something major happened. They'd be cut off from all communications with each other *and* the Joint Special Operations Command.

After the debrief, Wolf and the rest of his team were sitting around, killing time, waiting for darkness to fall and for the camp to quiet down, when Benny brought up their trackers.

"I've learned the hard way, and just wanted to touch base before we do this tonight. God forbid those ISIS assholes get ahold of any of us. Everyone got your trackers?"

Everyone nodded, but Mozart suddenly looked guilty.

"What the fuck?" Wolf asked in a stifled, rough voice. "I thought we agreed on this."

"We did, but honestly, with getting April and Summer settled and saying goodbye that morning, I simply forgot to grab it on my way out," Mozart defended himself. "It's usually in my tactical bag, but I took it out when we went on that one training exercise. It was stupid, I know."

Abe sighed. "Okay, it's not the end of the world. I'll stick to Mozart. Tex will have known we only had five trackers between the six of us from the moment we left. We got this."

The guys had given in reluctantly to their women's request to wear a tracker while they were on missions. After Benny had been kidnapped, and the fact that Tex's inability to track him led to Jess sacrificing herself and letting herself get taken as well, simply because she knew the tracker *she* was wearing would lead Tex right to Benny, they'd agreed to wear the GPS devices. The men had balked at first, saying their missions were highly classified, but Caroline had run roughshod over any and all of their arguments, correctly stating that Tex had the same security clearance as the rest of the team and he'd be the only one who would see where they were. She'd had a point, and eventually the guys agreed the extra security and peace of mind the trackers would give them, and their women, was worth it.

It wasn't the first time one of the guys had forgotten the small GPS tracking device, but this was the first time any of them thought it might just be a necessity.

ISIS didn't follow any rules of engagement. They were a ruthless gang of thugs who used the excuse of religion to torture and kill anyone they felt would further their cause. Not only would the team be up against a dangerous group of men, they'd be trying to snatch a prized possession right out from under the terrorists' noses. The probability was high they'd get separated in the chaos of the rescue and the trackers would've made everyone feel better about that possibility.

Wanting to lighten the mood, and change the subject away from his faux pas, Mozart asked, "Dude, what names are you guys considering for your little girl?"

"Honestly? I don't give a fuck. As long as she's alive and kicking, I couldn't care less."

"Really? So if Cheyenne names her Bertha, you're good with it?"

"Yup. She's gonna be my little cupcake no matter what name Cheyenne gives her." A few years ago, all the men would've given Dude no end of shit for his statement, but now, with families of their own? They got it. Dude continued, "I love egging Shy on though, so I've messed with her head so much, she doesn't know what she wants anymore."

"Not sure that's cool, honestly," Benny said. "Names are important, and if you've confused Cheyenne about what you want to name the baby versus what she wants to name her, that can be really stressful. I should know. Jess and I went back and forth and finally decided to give our kids as normal as names as possible. John and Sara are strong names and ones they won't be made fun of for."

"Like you were?" Wolf asked.

"Yeah. There weren't too many Kasons around when I was growing up, hell, even now, and it made my life hell."

"Shy knows I'm teasing her, Benny," Dude said seriously. "I wouldn't do one thing to cause Cheyenne more stress than she's already under. We laugh about it together. We see who can come up with the most ridiculous name. But we've had some serious conversations about it too. Any stress Shy has about naming our baby, she's bringing about on her own. Believe me, I've threatened to paddle her ass if she didn't stop vacillating back and forth, but she swears she wants to *see* our daughter before she picks a name. That she wants to make sure the name she has in her head matches what she sees when she looks at her face for the first time."

The men were quiet. They all knew Dude, knew he liked control, and knew any paddling he gave his wife would end in both their pleasure. They understood he'd never do anything purposely to hurt Cheyenne, just as any of them wouldn't hurt their wives.

"Sorry, man, I know you wouldn't hurt her. It's just—"

Dude cut Benny off. "It's cool. I get it. I just hope like fuck this can be done so I can be with her when it's time."

The men nodded. They all hoped so too, although

before tonight, they hadn't expected it to happen.

"Speaking of names," Cookie started with a grin, "you told your woman how you got your nickname yet, Benny?"

"Hell no," Benny immediately responded. "One, Jess would probably laugh her head off and I'd never hear the end of it, and two, there's no way in hell I ever want her knowing a prostitute somewhere in the depths of Africa gave that nickname to me."

The guys laughed quietly.

"This sounds like a good story," Rex said when the laughter had died down.

Abe didn't give Benny a chance to deflect the unasked question. "We were chilling out at a bar after a mission in Africa. A prostitute came up to our table to try to score for the night. She asked our man here if he was looking for a good time. Benny, thinking he was being witty, said, 'Been there, done that, got the T-shirt.' It was noisy in the bar and the prostitute didn't understand English that well and thought he was telling her his name. So she said, 'Ten Dollars for you, Benny Dunhat with the T-shirt.' It stuck."

Now it was the Virginia team's turn to laugh uproariously.

"Fucking classic," Rex said, and nodded approvingly.

"Assholes," Benny said putting his hands behind his

head and trying to relax back into his bedroll. "If Jess finds out, I'm holding you all responsible. I like the way she tries to convince me to tell her the story."

His teammates all laughed, but Benny knew if they'd kept their mouths shut for the last two years, he was good. They might make fun of him, but Benny knew it was all good-natured teasing. He didn't really care if Jess knew how he'd gotten his nickname, of course she and the other women knew prostitutes existed, but the more the girls asked, the more it became an ongoing inside joke with the guys. They all knew it drove the women nuts not to know the origin of Benny's nickname, and that made it all the more fun to keep it from them.

The tent quieted down, except for the regular noises of the camp settling in for the night around them. Rex's team had talked together quietly for a while, but now the men were slowly getting into battle mode. It was almost time.

PENELOPE SAT AGAINST one side of the tent thinking about what she wanted to eat first, after she drank a gallon of cold, clean water, when she got back to the States. A double-meat hamburger from *Whataburger*. No, that lava desert thing from *Chili's*. Hell, she didn't care. As long as it was big and she could eat until she felt like she would burst. That was what was most important.

She was in the middle of dreaming about food when she heard something. A bang sounded off to the east of her tent. It wasn't terribly loud, but it was enough to get her attention.

She heard two men speaking frantically in Arabic outside her tent, but no one entered. A little while later, Penelope heard a noise she'd dreamed about, but had started to think she'd never really hear.

The sound of the thick canvas material that made up the walls of her prison tearing. It could've been a terrorist or other bad guy coming to get her, but she didn't think so. They'd simply barge in the flap in the front, not try to be stealthy in the back. It had to be the cavalry.

Penelope turned to the sound and saw a black shape entering the tent from a large slice made in the back side of the tent.

"It's about fucking time," she said slowly and with extreme emotion, standing up and facing the shape, being cautious because there was still a *chance* it could be someone in the camp there to cause trouble.

Dude stood up inside the tent and looked at Sergeant Penelope Turner. She looked exactly like their intel said she'd look, albeit a little worse for the wear. Her blonde hair hung lanky around her shoulders and she looked as if she'd lost at least twenty pounds she couldn't spare. She wasn't very tall; the five-foot-two description was probably right on.

She stood in front of him, waiting for him to say something, more thankful than she could ever express he was there.

"United States Navy SEAL, Sergeant. We're here to take you home," Dude said in a muted tone.

"Awesome. I don't care if you're the President of the United States, as long as you're here to get me the fuck out of here."

Dude almost smiled. The team had a long discussion about the condition in which they might find this woman when they entered the tent. He'd been ready for anything, including resistance, but was more than happy to see she wasn't broken. Hell, she didn't even look bent.

"Any chance you have a weapon for me?"

Dude frowned down at her. "Can you handle it?" At her immediate scowl, he clarified, "I meant, you probably haven't eaten a whole lot. We have a ways to go to get to the extraction point. We don't exactly need you dropping it or losing control of it if we run into trouble." He watched as she thought through his words and his respect for her grew.

"Fuck. Yeah, you're probably right. I feel shaky as hell and I'm not sure how far I can go on my own steam. Got any water?" Penelope was frustrated that the SEAL thought she couldn't handle a pistol, but knew deep down he was probably right to be cautious. The last thing she wanted was to be a liability and somehow screw up her own rescue.

"We've got to get out of here, but as soon as we can find a safe spot and we're a good distance away, I'll make sure you get some water."

Penelope nodded. It was what she'd expected, and she'd prefer to get the hell out of there right now, rather than to take a drink and possibly get caught, but she was extremely thirsty and couldn't help the question from coming out anyway. She gestured to the slice in the tent. "Are you leading, or am I?"

Dude allowed his smile to come out this time. Damn, she was feisty. She reminded him a lot of his Shy. He gestured for her to go first. "I've got a man right outside, don't trip over him."

The look she gave him clearly told him to fuck off. He smiled again and watched as she carefully parted the material and took her first step toward freedom.

THE TRIP THROUGH the quiet, dark camp was surprisingly anticlimactic. Wolf and Benny led the way, making sure to notify Cookie and Dude of any detours they needed to make, while Mozart and Abe had their backs, making sure they weren't followed or harassed as they made their way through the camp.

Rex's SEAL team had done their job well. They didn't encounter anyone suspicious and made good time toward the extraction point.

Penelope followed Dude as best she could. He'd stopped about ten minutes after they'd left the tent and given her a canteen of water. Penelope wanted to guzzle it down and then pour another over her head, but she controlled her urges and took only a few sips. The last thing she wanted to do was get sick in the middle of her rescue. She handed it back to the SEAL who had entered her tent and felt a warmth in her belly at the look of approval in his eyes. It had been so long since anyone had looked at her with respect, it felt good. She shrugged it off and did what she usually did, said something snarky, simply to get through the moment without crying. "If you're done eyeballin' me, how 'bout we get out of this fucking desert?"

But instead of pissing him off, which was what her comebacks usually did, he merely smiled and nodded at her, then at the SEAL behind her, and set off again.

Just when Penelope didn't think she could take another step, they stopped and the SEAL in front of her gestured for her to crouch down. She couldn't see much; it was darker than ever with no moon to help illuminate their path. She'd made her way through the camp with one hand on the SEAL's back or tucked into his vest. She kneeled down and strained to see something, anything.

"In about three minutes, an MH-60 Blackhawk is gonna scream in here from the north. Keep your eyes closed as it comes in so you don't get any sand in them, and whatever you do, don't let go of my vest. Got it?"

"How will *you* be able to see?" Penelope had never been one to blindly follow orders, even back home at the firehouse.

"I've got night-vision goggles on, they'll shield my eyes from the blowing sand and dirt. You're gonna have to run. Can you do that? And be honest."

Penelope tried to look up at the man, but dammit, it was still too dark to clearly see him. She thought about it. Could she run? The walk across the camp had almost done her in. But run to freedom? Hell yeah, she could do it. "Yes." She didn't elaborate.

"All right. If for any reason you think you can't make it to the chopper, pull down hard on my vest. I'll get your ass there. We aren't leaving this fucking desert without you, Sergeant. No way in hell."

Penelope felt the tears gather in her eyes. Crap. No. She couldn't break down. Not now. Not when she was so close to freedom. "Thank you." She paused, then asked, "What was your name again?"

"Dude. And that's Cookie behind you. I don't know

if you'll remember or not, but Wolf and Benny cleared the way ahead of us as we went through camp, and Mozart and Abe brought up the rear. We'll all pile in the chopper with you, so once we get there, scoot your ass in as far as you can. You know the MH-60?"

"Yeah," Penelope told him, impressed with his professionalism and his abilities so far. "Holds ten comfortably in the back. Pilot, copilot, gunner, and crew chief in the front."

"You know the MH-60." This time it wasn't a question.

Penelope smiled, loving when she could surprise people. It happened all the time because people judged her based on her size and her looks. It was nice, for the first time in a long few months, to be treated as if she was an equal.

"Brace." Dude's voice was quiet, and Penelope braced. Within seconds she heard the hum of the rotors of the chopper. Before she'd joined the military, she'd only been familiar with single-rotor helicopters that were mostly used by hospitals and ambulance services. Because of the single rotor, they made the stereotypical whap-whap-whap sound. The MH-60 was a more powerful and bigger chopper and thus had several blades on the rotor. She'd never heard anything so wonderful before in her life as that helicopter hovering overhead in the dark night.

The chopper was flying low and with no lights. It entered the clearing and lowered until it was hovering inches from the ground.

"Let's go. Now!" Dude said.

Penelope felt him stand up as she'd already grabbed on to his vest and her eyes popped open. They were running toward the huge machine before she could think. She tripped once, but her grip on the SEAL's vest kept her from face-planting into the unforgiving desert floor. She got her feet under her and continued running as if the hounds of hell were at her heels. She felt a hand on her back and didn't have to look back to know it was the other SEAL who had been by her side throughout their journey out of the camp.

They arrived at the open bay door on the right side of the chopper and a man, most likely the crew chief, was there with his hand outstretched, ready to help them in.

Penelope let go of the vest she was holding and Dude leaped into the cargo area. He immediately turned to help her up. She threw both hands upward and felt the men already in the helicopter grab hold of her hands and there was a hand on her butt that boosted her up at the same time. She immediately moved away from the open door when her hands were let go, scrabbling back on her hands and knees.

She watched as five more dark shapes leaped

onboard the helicopter with only minimal help from Dude. The crew chief went back up to his seat on the right side of the chopper and Penelope felt the machine rising into the air about two seconds after the last SEAL leaped into the cargo area.

With the seven of them in the space, it suddenly seemed smaller than when she'd first been hauled aboard. There wasn't time to strap into any seats so Penelope crab-walked backwards until she felt her spine hit something solid. She braced herself and held on as the helicopter raced off into the black night.

# Chapter Ten

*"Cade, your sister has been missing for over three months now. Do you think you'll ever see her again?"*

*"Yes, absolutely."*

*"How can you be sure?"*

*"How can anyone be sure of anything? My sister is a fighter, but more than that, she's smart. You've seen her on those videos, everyone in America has seen her. She does exactly what she's told to do, and it's kept her alive this long. Those* BLEEP *are keeping her alive to use her. She's pretty, and they're using her as a propaganda tool. All she needs is for the government to send someone in to get her. Knowing her, she'll probably complain to their faces about how long it took them to find her and get her out."*

*"The government has said time and time again that they don't negotiate with terrorists, do you really think they're going to spend possibly millions of dollars, and risk countless lives, to send a team in to*

*rescue her?"*

*"First of all, there aren't any negotiations needed. They can go in and steal her back. Second of all, I can't believe you're putting a price on my sister's head. She's an American soldier. She put her life on the line when she was sent over there in the first place. The United States government sent her there, they can damn well go and get her back."*

*"What will be the first words you say to your sister if you see her again?"*

"When *I see her, I'll tell her I love her and that I never gave up trying to find her."*

*The reporter faced the camera for the first time and said to the viewing audience, "In case you missed it before, here's the last tape that has been released of Sergeant Turner reading a message from the ISIS terrorists..."*

FIONA SAT WITH MELODY and they watched as Akilah played with little Sara. Jessyka was glad to let Fiona babysit her toddler for a while. It was a good break for both mother and daughter. Akilah didn't speak perfect English yet, but neither did the two-year-old, so they actually entertained each other very easily.

"I'm so proud of you and Tex for adopting Akilah."

"*I'm* glad Tex was able to make arrangements so quickly so we *could* adopt her."

"Does it ever bother you that Tex can…make things happen…so easily?"

Melody knew what Fiona was asking. "You know what? I trust Tex explicitly. He's too damn honest to do anything for himself, or us, illegally."

Fiona laughed, catching the "or us" that Melody threw in there. "Well, I know you know this, but Tex holds a special place in my heart. I'd do anything for him and I'm thrilled knowing you guys found each other."

"*He* found *me*, you mean," Melody corrected.

"Yeah, that's what I meant. We've always said Tex could find anyone, and of course we were right." Fiona noticed that Melody's gaze was on her daughter. She looked over and saw that Akilah was watching the television with rapt attention. She looked at the screen and saw the last video of the poor American soldier that had been made public had just finished playing.

"What is it, Akilah?" Melody asked softly.

Akilah just shrugged and went back to playing with Sara. Melody and Fiona looked at each other again.

"Is she really okay? I can't imagine what sorts of things she witnessed over in Iraq," Fiona asked in a low voice.

"I think so. Sometimes I'll catch her staring off into space, but she always smiles at me and says she's fine when I ask if she's all right."

"Do you think she misses it?"

"Sometimes, yeah. It'd be like us suddenly moving to Germany and not speaking German. We could acclimate, but sometimes we'd long for a *McDonald's* burger…you know?"

Fiona did understand, better than she figured Melody thought after spending all that time in Mexico when she'd been kidnapped. Surprisingly, having Julie living in the same town was cathartic. Having someone who Fiona could talk to about what they went through, and knowing that the other woman honestly understood where she was coming from and what she was feeling, was a relief. While she and Julie didn't hang out all the time, they'd come far enough in their relationship to actually call themselves friends and go out every now and then for lunch.

They visited for a while longer and finally Melody figured it was time to head back to Caroline's. They were all going to try to meet at *Aces* for dinner, and Melody knew Akilah would need a mental break before they headed out to meet in a big group like that. She was doing really well, but Melody didn't want to push it.

They were in Caroline's car that she let them borrow and on their way back to Caroline's house when Akilah asked from the backseat, "What was TV about?"

Melody looked up at the rearview mirror at her daughter, feeling lucky for the millionth time that she was in her and Tex's life. She tried to explain without getting into too much detail. Akilah was only twelve, but she'd seen enough that she sometimes acted thirty. Melody wanted to keep her as young as possible for as long as possible. "An American soldier was kidnapped by ISIS."

"She on video?

"Yes, people think that is her."

Akilah was silent for a while then said, bizarrely, "I speak Arabic."

"Yes, honey, I know you do."

"There was Arabic on TV."

Melody looked sharply at her daughter. "Yes, I saw some men in the background talking. You know what they were saying?"

Akilah didn't look happy. "Yes."

"Did you hear them?"

"No. Lips."

"You could read their lips? And they were speaking in Arabic?"

Akilah nodded, eyes wide.

"Was it something bad?"

"Yes."

"Do you need to tell Tex?"

Akilah looked out the window and thought about what to tell Melody. She might only be twelve years old, but she knew enough about her new father to know he was different from the other fathers in the special school she attended. She knew Tex was like her, missing a limb, but also because he talked to her one night about what it was he did. He'd been honest, and Akilah understood most of it. He used his computers to help people. He found people who were lost, he did research to help the American soldiers and the American government, and he could…she didn't know what the strange phrase meant when Tex had told her, but she remembered the phrase and figured it meant he could do special things other people couldn't. All because of his computer.

Pull strings. That's the funny American saying he'd used. If her new dad could pull these strings and help the poor American woman who was lost and who had a horrible accent when she'd been reading the few Arabic words on the letter, then she needed to tell him what she'd heard.

"Yes," Akilah said solemnly.

"Okay. We'll call him when we get to Caroline's house."

Akilah sat back and relaxed a little bit. She was very happy Melody treated her as if she was important. When she spoke, Melody listened, unlike back in her country, where many times women's opinions and thoughts were dismissed or ignored. It made her feel good inside, happy to be here in America with her new family. She wanted to help in any way she could.

# Chapter Eleven

SOMEONE HANDED PENELOPE a set of headphones. She could hear the pilots talking to each other in muted voices, and every now and then one of the SEALs would say something to another. But she kept silent. She was so very thankful she was alive and away from the damn kidnappers. If she stopped to think for one second about what she'd just lived through, she knew she'd be a basket-case.

Penelope also didn't want to think right now about that poor Australian soldier, or Thomas, Henry, and Robert. She'd remember their lives, and deaths, at another time and another place; this wasn't it. While she was thankful to be away from the refugee camp, she'd overheard enough from the pilots and the SEALs to know they weren't completely out of danger.

While she'd been in the hands of ISIS, there wasn't one moment that went by that she didn't feel scared because she was a female in the midst of a male dominated society, and one that was definitely anti-woman.

She'd known at any time she could be raped, or passed around to each of the terrorists. God only knew why they'd left her alone all these months. She thought she remembered reading one time that blonde-haired women were somehow regarded suspiciously in the Muslim culture, but she could've been making that up. Whatever the reason, she was more thankful than she thought she could even express.

But right now, in this helicopter, surrounded by ten very masculine men…men who could easily hold her down and do whatever they wanted with her, she wasn't scared at all. First, these were American soldiers; second, they'd come to rescue her. Third, she could sense, at least with the SEALs, they oozed honor and protectiveness from their very bones. She was safe with them. Utterly and completely safe. Penelope was dehydrated and hungry, and had been beaten up more than once, but she was here and alive and, for the moment, safe. She'd take it.

Penelope was just starting to relax into a kind of half-asleep/half-awake state, when she heard one of the pilots swear through the headphones she was wearing.

"Fucking hell. Brace, brace, brace! Incoming!"

Those were the last words she remembered hearing before the chopper lurched after a large explosion and everything went black.

# Chapter Twelve

"HEY, TEX. IT'S me. Please call me back as soon as you can. I know you're holed up in your cave, but this is important. Akilah needs to tell you what she saw on the news. She was watching a clip of that kidnapped woman soldier reading something, and she saw some men in the background speaking Arabic. Apparently she read their lips, and she won't tell me what they said, but she did admit that you needed to know. Please. Call me as soon as you can."

Melody hung up the phone and sighed. Short of doing something underhanded, like putting her tracker in a Dumpster and letting it get carried to the landfill, which would certainly get her husband's attention, she didn't know what to do. He was usually very protective of both her and Akilah, but with everything else that had been going on it was possible he'd lost track of time. Eventually he'd come out of his cave to shower, or eat, and he'd notice she'd left a message both on his cell phone and on their ancient house phone.

In the meantime, she did what she could to help out her friends. Jess was feeling frazzled with not only her two kids, but the "afternoon sickness," as she called it. Alabama was doing fine with Brinique and Davisa, but the two girls were feeling clingy since Christopher had left. Summer was good, glowing and fully recovered after April's birth, but she was struggling with being back at work and away from April all day after her maternity leave was up.

Melody knew Caroline was worried about Fiona. She hadn't been around much, because she'd been working so hard, and everyone always worried about her when their men were off on a mission. And finally there was Cheyenne. Caroline had tried to get her to sleep at her house, so if she needed to go have her baby in the middle of the night, Caroline would be there to help, but so far she'd refused, saying she was fine and didn't want to get in anyone's way.

Melody, as always, was impressed with Caroline. The woman took a lot on, but honestly seemed to thrive on it. She could work a full shift at the lab, then come home, babysit, give advice, and even host a dinner get-together for all the women and their kids…and still come out on the other side smiling.

She went into the kitchen to see Caroline teaching Akilah how to make cookies from scratch. Akilah was obsessed with cooking. Anytime she ate something she enjoyed, she'd ask how to make it and bug Melody until they made the dish together. Melody figured it was because growing up in Iraq, food could be scarce, so she had no problem sharing what she knew with her new daughter. All too soon, Akilah would be a teenager and probably have no time for her mother.

Caroline's phone rang when she was wrist-deep in the middle of mixing the cookie dough by hand, which she insisted was the only way to make sure all the ingredients got mixed together properly. She'd even claimed her chemistry background proved it was true.

"I'll get it," Melody said as she reached for the phone. "Hello?"

"Caroline?"

"No, this is Melody. Cheyenne?"

"Yeah…uh…"

"Are you all right?"

Melody heard her panting on the other end of the line, then she said, "Yeah, but it's time."

"It's time? Baby time? Are you sure?"

"Yeah. I'm sure."

Melody held her hand over the phone and screeched to Caroline, "It's time!" Then she moved her hand and got back to Cheyenne. "Where are you? Have you called an ambulance? We're coming to get you."

"I'm still at home, I haven't called an ambulance yet…I called Caroline. But—"

"Okay, then we're on our way. Do you have your suitcase there with you? We can't forget that."

"I was calling to tell Caroline, but I'm about to call the ambulance. Can you guys meet me at the hospital?"

"Yeah, of course, but why don't we just come get you? That baby isn't going to come in the next ten minutes… Wait…is she?"

"No, I don't think so…but…I'm bleeding. It's not right."

"Shit, okay, I'm hanging up now. Call 911 immediately and we'll meet you at the hospital. I'm sure it's fine. Don't panic. All right?"

"Okay. Melody?"

"Yeah, Cheyenne?"

"I'm scared."

"It's going to be fine. Now, shut up, hang up, and call 911."

"Okay, see you soon."

Melody clicked off the phone and saw that Caroline had already washed her hands and was impatiently waiting to hear what was going on.

Melody shoved the phone at Caroline and reached in her back pocket for her own. "That was obviously Cheyenne. She's having the baby now, but she's bleeding. Damn woman called *you* before calling 911. I swear, cops and doctors and nurses, and apparently 911 operators, are always the last to call for help when they need it. You call Alabama and Fiona. I'll call Jessyka and Summer. We need to get to the hospital. Pronto."

Caroline nodded and immediately dialed. Operation Baby Cooper was happening. Now.

# Chapter Thirteen

PENELOPE CAME BACK to consciousness suddenly. She'd always read about how people gradually came back into themselves after being knocked out, but that wasn't the case with her.

She could smell aviation fuel and smoke from a fire. She opened her eyes and saw destruction all around her. Jesus.

She remembered now, the helicopter she'd been in had obviously crashed, or been shot down, more likely.

She looked around and saw nothing but rocks and scrub bushes. They were obviously in the mountains, but she had no idea what mountains or in what country. But first things first. Penelope's EMT training kicked in. She painfully got up on her hands and knees and paused, taking stock of herself.

Nothing seemed broken, except maybe a rib or two. She could function with that, no problem. It hurt like hell, but in the scope of her current situation, it was negligible. She also had cuts, scrapes, and probably a hell of a lot of bruises. All in all, she was in remarkable shape for falling out of the sky while inside a metal box.

Penelope looked around and saw three men lying near her. She crawled over and vaguely noticed they were three of the SEALs who had helped her escape. Penelope couldn't remember their names, but at the moment it didn't matter. All three were out cold but, when she checked, thankfully they were breathing. Taking a quick look at them, Penelope thought one had a broken arm—it was lying above his head at a weird angle—and the other two looked relatively whole. She couldn't tell if they had any kind of internal bleeding or head wounds though.

She looked up when she heard a noise. It was Dude, the man who'd appeared in her tent prison as if an angel from God.

"You good?" he asked gruffly. He was carrying one of the men from the helicopter, who didn't look good at all.

Penelope nodded. "I'm good. What can I do to help?"

Dude eyed the small woman carefully. They were in a world of hurt, and were fucked if they didn't get their shit together. He might as well use her as much as she'd be able to help him. He ignored the tweaks in his injured ankle and told her solemnly, "Copilot is dead. Gunner and crew chief are in bad shape. My teammates are generally all right, but have various injuries. The pilots did a hell of a job getting the bird down without killing us all. But we're fucked if we don't get the hell out of here." Dude waited for Penelope to nod, and continued. "I'll get everyone out here, but I need your help in triaging them. Can you do that?"

"Yes. I'm an EMT back home in Texas. I'll do my best."

"Thank you." The two words were short and heartfelt.

Penelope nodded and turned back to the men who were in front of her. She looked around and saw a red bag with a white cross on it. At one time, she would've questioned how it was right where she needed it to be at exactly the right moment, but after seeing more than one miracle as a firefighter and EMT, now she took them in stride. She made her way over to the first-aid kit and dragged it back to the SEALs. She saw one of the men's eyes were open and he was watching her intently.

"Hi, remember me? I'm Penelope and I'm going to help you." She fell into emergency medical technician mode automatically. This was something she was familiar with. "Are you all right? Does anything hurt?"

She watched the man take stock of himself. He moved his legs slowly, then each arm, and finally he rotated his head back and forth. "I think I'm in one piece. Everything hurts, but nothing's broken. Sit rep?"

Penelope sighed in relief. Thank God he was alive. One man's condition known, seven to go. She answered the SEAL. "From what I'm guessing, RPG took down the chopper. One dead, seven unknown."

"I'm Cookie. I wasn't sure if you remembered who I was."

"I didn't, and I can't promise to remember you later either, but thank you. Can you help me?" Penelope gestured to the man with the obviously broken arm who hadn't woken up yet.

"What do you need?"

"We need to set his arm. It's gonna hurt like hell and I'm not sure I can hold him if he wakes up in the middle of it."

"Fuck. Wolf is not going to be happy about this."

"Wolf?"

"Yeah, this is Wolf, our team leader. And the man there," Cookie gestured to the other motionless man, "is Benny."

Penelope nodded and the two got to work. Cookie was also trained in first aid, probably more than she was since he was a SEAL, and they quickly were able to set Wolf's arm against his side, keeping it immobile. He was just coming around when Dude came back to them with the pilot. He had a large wound on his head and was bleeding profusely.

"Pilot's in bad shape. I'm not sure we can move any

of the Night Stalkers." His words were directed at Cookie.

Cookie nodded. "Let me help you get the others and we'll go to Plan D."

The two men left to go back toward the wrecked hunk of metal that used to be an MH-60 helicopter and Penelope turned to Benny. Cookie and Dude returned quickly, each carrying another one of the men from the helicopter crew.

"Mozart's coming around in the chopper. He's got a large gash on his upper arm, but is otherwise whole. Where's Abe?"

"Shit. He's the only one unaccounted for."

Penelope suddenly felt weighed down with guilt. She sat back on her heels and looked at the six men lying broken on the ground in front of her. Damn.

"This is not your fucking fault."

Penelope turned and looked at the man with the broken arm, Wolf, who'd spoken. "How do you know what I was thinking?" she asked in surprise.

"It's written all over your face, sweetheart."

"I don't think you're allowed to call me sweetheart."

Wolf laughed. Actually laughed. "Sorry, when you're about as big as a bug and as cute as a button, don't think I can call you anything *but* sweetheart, regardless of your rank and obvious competence as a soldier."

"Are you fucking kidding me? That's the most sexist thing I've heard since I've been in this country, and that's saying something," Penelope groused at Wolf.

He laughed again upon seeing her glare. "Sorry. Help me sit up." Now *that* actually sounded like a command.

Penelope helped ease him to a sitting position. "That arm's gonna hurt like hell. We gave you some morphine, but not a lot. Cookie didn't think you should be loopy when we try to outrun insurgents in the fucking mountains…his words, not mine."

Wolf nodded. "How're they?" It was as if his earlier words hadn't been spoken. Penelope was much more comfortable with this no-nonsense, sticking to the details conversation.

"Copilot's dead. I haven't gotten to the other three men. I can't see anything wrong with…Benny, I think the others called him, and they're off looking for Abe. Dude is limping a bit, but he's acting impervious to pain, so it's probably not too bad. Mozart seems to be okay and will probably drag his carcass over here soon; again, their words, not mine."

Wolf scooted toward the unconscious Army pilots as Penelope did the same. They worked in silence, Wolf helping her bandage where he could and offering suggestions. They heard noises in the shrubs behind them and before Penelope could think, Wolf had turned and aimed a pistol in the direction of the footsteps.

"Easy, Wolf, it's us," Penelope heard, right before three SEALs emerged from the dense underbrush.

The man they'd called Abe was walking…sort of. There was blood on the bottom of his pants and it was obvious, if not for the help from his teammates, he wouldn't be mobile at all.

"Fuck, Abe, what'd you go and do?"

Dude answered for him. "We pulled a nice-sized chunk of metal out of his thigh. We field dressed it, but it's gonna need stitches when we get to where we're going."

They set Abe down on the ground next to Benny, who was finally coming around. Upon further examination, Benny was all right. He had a raging headache but no open head wound, which, unfortunately, meant he probably had a concussion. Mozart walked into their midst, wobbling a bit but upright and mobile. It was something, at least.

"Plan D discussion," Wolf said in a quiet, serious voice. "Sergeant Turner, listen up, you're a part of this team now too."

Penelope nodded, glad they weren't going to try to shove her off to the side while they made all the decisions. She had a sudden *need* to know what was going on. She'd been kept in the dark about everything for the last few months. It felt good to be included.

"Abe's out with that leg, and that means he'll need two of us to help him. I've got a broken arm, Benny has a concussion. Mozart is moving, but that arm is gonna be about as useless as mine. Tiger here is favoring her right side, so I'm assuming she's got some sort of broken or cracked ribs."

"Wait, what? Tiger?" Penelope wasn't sure she liked that nickname, although it was a hell of a lot better than what the guys back at the firehouse called her.

"Fierce as a fucking tiger," Wolf said without even a smile. He continued as if she hadn't interrupted him. "So that leaves us with Dude and Cookie relatively unscathed, but you guys will need to help Abe." He looked sadly at the Night Stalkers. "We can't take them with us."

The men were silent for a moment, then Benny said, "Our trackers. We've got five of them. If we leave one on each of them, Tex can track 'em."

"What's the radio situation?" Abe asked.

Cookie shook his head in response. "No radios. They're dead. I agree with Benny. We can't take them with us, but we can't leave them at the mercy of the insurgents either," he said.

"What?" Penelope felt like a broken record. "The radios are dead? And trackers? What trackers?"

"No time to fully explain, but in a nutshell, five of us have GPS trackers on us that are being monitored by the best fucking hacker I've ever met in my life. He's got our back at all times, including while we're on missions," Mozart told her.

"That's not legal is it?"

"Who the fuck cares? Right now it's all these guys have. It's their only chance to get out of this fucking country with their heads attached," Benny said somewhat bitterly.

Penelope winced. Dammit. He was right. "But the copilot? He's already dead—"

Wolf didn't let her finish. "A SEAL doesn't leave a SEAL behind, ever. He might be dead, and there's a chance the insurgents will ignore his body and leave him alone, but if they decide to take him somewhere and desecrate his body for one of their fucking videos, he'll hopefully be able to be found before that can happen. We'll leave the trackers with the others as well. If the insurgents get their hands on them there's a possibility they could be separated, so each of them having a tracker will make it easier for the cavalry to find them."

Penelope gulped. Okay, she got it. These men were loyal to the core, and it didn't matter that the Night Stalkers were Army, not Navy. They'd come to get her out, and had refused to leave her behind as well. Just the type of soldiers she wanted to be around. "Right."

Cookie walked to Wolf, Abe, and Benny, and collected their trackers. While he was busy planting them on the other men, Penelope asked. "Why only five when there are six of you?"

It was Mozart who answered without hesitating. "Because I was the dumbass who forgot it. You can bet my wife will kick my ass when I get home. Believe me, I'm kicking my own ass right about now."

Penelope watched as Cookie spoke to each of the injured men, obviously explaining what was going on. His face was serious and grim when he returned.

"Okay, here's the deal. The pilot said the RPG came from the southeast. We're too far from Yuksekova to get to the base on foot. We're in the middle of the Hakkari Daglari mountain range, which separates Iraq and Turkey. Our best bet at this point is to find a good place to hunker down and wait them out. We need to take the high ground if we're gonna have any chance of surviving an onslaught by ISIS or Al Qaeda. Tex will know where we went down and will most likely get with JSOC. They should send in Delta Force or even Rex's SEAL team. We don't have a lot of time, but Benny and I will move the injured Night Stalkers to safer ground, and then the seven of us will bug out of here. We'll head up into the mountains where there's a large cave system."

"But aren't the caves where the insurgents generally hole up?" Penelope asked uncertainly.

Cookie merely shrugged and nodded.

"How are we gonna avoid them?"

"Luck."

Penelope growled. She definitely didn't like the answers she was getting. "Wouldn't it be better to stay here with the pilots and let your friend do his thing? If anyone comes we can fight them off defensively here."

Wolf didn't get angry over her disagreement, but his words were impatient, as if he knew they were running out of time. "Cookie, Benny, go ahead and move the others. We'll prepare what we can while you're gone." He turned to Penelope to answer her question. "We can't defend this position. Look around, we're in a hole. We need to get up high to have a good vantage point. We're sitting ducks here. We still have Dude's tracker, Tex will know something's up, and will be able to find us."

"But..." Penelope looked at the men Dude and Cookie were currently helping take a more defensive position. "Do they know about how hard it is to defend this position?"

Wolf nodded grimly.

Holy freaking shit. Penelope swallowed hard once. Then twice. By agreeing to stay, by not demanding to go with them, the men were basically signing their death warrants. But if they insisted on going with them, they were *all* in grave danger.

Wolf's voice was subdued and gentle, if not sad at the same time. "The gunner has two broken legs. The crew chief hasn't regained consciousness and is bleeding out of his ears and nose. The pilot broke both ankles and both wrists in the crash. With our injuries we can't carry them. They know the odds, Tiger. I'm just thankful we can leave the trackers with them. It'll give them a better shot than if they didn't have them."

Penelope abruptly turned away and started to gather as much gear as she could find, and that she thought they'd need. She knew she'd see those men's faces and hear their voices in her dreams for years to come. She made a vow to herself, to make sure every American knew what a huge sacrifice they'd made and how brave they'd been in the face of certain death.

She felt a hand on her forearm and looked up. It was Dude.

"Tex will find them. He'll get them home to their families. He'll find them, and the cavalry will find *us*."

Penelope nodded, knowing if she opened her mouth she'd embarrass herself by bursting into tears. There was only so much a girl could take, and she'd about reached the end of her rope.

Cookie, Dude, Wolf, Mozart, and Penelope gathered as much as they could easily carry, being sure to take as much ammo and as many firearms as possible. Penelope didn't say a word as Dude handed her a KA-BAR knife and a loaded pistol. She nodded at him in thanks, remembering their conversation from back in the tent, and they got ready to leave. She wasn't in any better shape than she was when she'd been rescued from the tent city, but the game had changed. She was a vital part of the team now, and as one of the least wounded amongst them, she had to carry her weight.

Wolf led the way, with Dude and Cookie supporting Abe on either side, following him. Benny was next, then Mozart, and finally Penelope. She was aware of the significance of being last in the line. It was her responsibility to have their sixes, their asses. It wasn't something she took lightly. She'd pull her weight with these men or die trying. Her brother hadn't browbeat and nagged her into passing the firefighter certification test for nothing. She was a Turner, she wouldn't let them down.

As they headed up into the mountains, Penelope took one more look back before they went over a rise. She could see the black smoke rising up from the wreckage of the chopper, a beacon for any and all insurgents in the area. She couldn't see the pilot and the other men, but knew they were there in the shadows, waiting to fight, and possibly die.

The thought was too much. She allowed the tears to fall as she walked, knowing the SEALs in front of her were too preoccupied to notice.

# Chapter Fourteen

*In world news today, a source at the White House has confirmed the crash of an MH-60 helicopter in the Hakkari Daglari mountain range, between Turkey and Iraq. There's no word of injuries or how many were onboard, but speculation is that the occupants were either on their way to attempt to rescue kidnapped American soldier, Penelope Turner, or were returning after an attempt. No word on if the rescue was attempted or if it was successful, and there is no information on casualties from the crash. Stay tuned for an update on the ten o'clock news.*

MELODY LOOKED DOWN at the vibrating phone in her hand. Thank freaking God. "Hello?"

"Cheyenne is having the baby?"

Melody wasn't surprised Tex knew they were all at the hospital and the only reason—well, the only good reason—was because Cheyenne was in labor. "Yeah, she was bleeding when her water broke and we convinced her to call 911. She finally did and we're all here waiting now."

"I got your message. I'm sorry I didn't answer when you called. I promise I'm trying to get better at making sure I keep my phone with me and on," Tex apologized.

"I know you are. Is…everything okay?" Melody had seen the news, there wasn't any way to avoid it.

"Is Akilah there? I don't have a lot of time."

Well shit. If he wasn't answering her, everything wasn't all right. She didn't protest, or ask any more questions. "Yeah, she's here, hang on…okay?"

"Of course. Mel?"

Melody paused mid-turn toward her daughter. "Yeah, Tex?"

"I love you. I love you more than I've ever loved anyone or anything in my life. You know that, right?"

Man oh man oh man. Something was terribly wrong. Thinking back to the newscast about the crashed helicopter, Melody's mouth got dry and she felt as if she was going to throw up. She wasn't going to ask though. There was no way she'd be able to keep something like that from her friends, so she didn't want to know. Besides, Cheyenne was about to have a baby. This was no time to bring any heartache or worries into the mix.

"I love you too, Tex. To Vegas and back." It was their saying. Ever since they'd driven across the country twice, the second time to get married, it had become their thing.

"Get Akilah for me. Stay safe. Love you."

"I will. Love you too. Hang on." Melody turned and gestured to Akilah, who'd had her eyes on her probably the entire time she'd been speaking to Tex. She held out the phone to the twelve-year-old. "It's Tex," she said in a soft voice. "Tell him what you saw on the TV."

Akilah took the phone and nodded and walked out to the main reception room and outside the hospital doors. "Hello?"

"Hi, sweetie. Mel says you heard something?"

"Read words on television in Arabic."

Tex had gotten used to reading between the lines when it came to Akilah's broken English. She'd gotten much better over the last few months, but especially over the phone, he had to help her find the right words. "You were watching the news and someone was speaking Arabic and you could tell what they said by reading their lips?"

"Yes."

"What did they say?"

"Lady was reading letter in English. Man in black standing behind. Turned and talk to other man."

"Okay, go on."

"Said wanted to take more Americans."

"Take? Like the female soldier?"

"Yes. Said now was good time. Lots of soldiers in camp."

This wasn't huge news to Tex, he knew the government was well aware ISIS wanted to kidnap and torture as many English speaking soldiers as possible, but he was still impressed with his daughter. "Anything else?"

"No."

"Thank you, Akilah. You are amazing."

"I help?"

"You helped a lot."

Akilah smiled. She enjoyed feeling useful. Tex and Melody always made sure they told her how proud they were of her and how happy they were she was with them. "Miss you."

"Oh, sweetie, I miss you too. Tell Mel to get you guys home soon. Yeah?"

"Okay."

"Take care of Melody for me. I love you."

"I will. Love you too."

Tex smiled broadly on the other side of the country. He thought that was the first time Akilah had said the words. He didn't want to make a big deal out of it though, it might embarrass her and she'd be reluctant to say them again in the future. "I'll talk to you later. If you hear or read anything else on the news, call me right away."

"Yes."

"Okay, talk to you later."

"Bye."

"Bye, Akilah."

Tex hung up the phone and turned back to the bank of computer screens in front of him. He'd known the helicopter had crashed the second it'd gone down. The program that tracked his friends was up and he'd watched as the red dots suddenly stopped moving well before they'd reached the Special Forces base at Yuksekova. When there were four dots which stayed put and one which started up the mountains, Tex knew they were in trouble. Splitting up wasn't standard operating procedure. He'd immediately reached out to his contacts and given them the coordinates of where those four dots were.

He'd been informed that JSOC was putting together a Delta Force team at that very moment to head into the mountains to get his friends. Tex's information would cut their search time dramatically, but he was glad to hear they were already aware something had gone wrong and were heading out on the rescue mission.

What they'd find when they got there was anyone's guess. Tex had no idea who the four motionless trackers were attached to and he could only hope he wouldn't have to be telling his wife, or the women he'd come to love as sisters, that some of their men wouldn't be coming home alive.

# Chapter Fifteen

PENELOPE HAD BEEN good for the first hour of walking, adrenaline and nervousness propelling her on, but slowly, as they settled into the hike, her strength had waned. Lack of exercise, lack of proper nutrition, lack of enough good clean water, and some cracked ribs, it was all taking its toll.

But she felt better knowing she wasn't the only one. Apparently Abe wasn't light, and Cookie and Dude were having a hard time helping him get over the boulders and hills that were between them and the dubious safety of a hole in the side of a mountain. Abe was helping as much as he could, but the shrapnel in his thigh had done a number on him, and even with his help, it was slow going. Penelope had no idea how Wolf and the rest of the guys were going to decide *which* cave was the best for them, but she had no doubt that they'd find the perfect place.

One foot in front of the other was her mantra. She'd be damned if *she'd* be the reason they were held up. She felt guilty enough as it was for putting these men in this position in the first place. Oh, intellectually she knew that *she* hadn't done it, but there was no getting around the fact that they were all here, tromping through the mountains in Turkey, injured and most likely being hunted by insurgents, because they were sent to rescue her.

Penelope wiped away the sweat from her brow, thankful she'd gotten enough liquid in her to be *able* to sweat, for what seemed the millionth time and trudged on. She finally saw Dude and Cookie ease Abe to the ground and sighed in relief. Thank freaking God. She honestly had no idea how much longer she could've continued.

"We'll stop here for the night. We can't stay here for good, but we've gone far enough. We all need the break. Abe, we'll get your leg properly sewed up and stuff you full of antibiotics. Mozart, same for you. Tiger, if you need those ribs wrapped, we'll do that as well."

"What about you, Wolf? How's the arm?" Penelope dared to ask, irritated when every single man grinned at her. "What? What's so fucking funny?" She was tired, hungry, thirsty, and her ribs hurt like hell. The last thing she appreciated were six hot guys laughing at her.

Mozart cleared his throat and was the first to speak. "Nothing's funny, Tiger. I suppose it's just that you remind us of our women. They're kind of like you.

Spunky and motherly all at the same time."

Penelope looked at them in horror. "I'm not motherly."

Everyone but Benny was able to hold back their laughter. Benny snorted in disbelief and he mocked her in a remarkably good imitation. "How's the arm, Wolf?"

"Shut up. Just because I'm a decent human being doesn't mean I'm motherly. Admit it, you all wanted to know as well."

"Well, yeah, but you were the one who said it," Abe joked through his pain.

Penelope rolled her eyes. "Fine. I hope his arm falls off, and your head, and your leg," she groused, looking at Wolf, Benny, and Abe respectively.

"Come on, we need to work to get this area ready for us to spend the night. It's not ideal, but it'll have to do," Wolf said, interrupting the light joking.

Cookie and Dude got to work putting together a makeshift bunk for each of them while at the same time concealing them as much as possible.

Penelope sat next to Abe and did her best to clean, sew, and bandage his leg. The wound was jagged and deep, and her stitches wouldn't win any awards by the Cosmetology Center of America, but she didn't think Abe cared. More important than her sewing skills, she hoped the antibiotic cream and the antibiotics he'd swallowed would stave off any infection.

Since everyone was exhausted, they settled down fairly quickly after coming up with a rotation for who would stay up first on watch. They decided to schedule the watch in pairs, to make sure no one fell asleep. The last thing they needed was an insurgent sneaking up on the camp because someone was too tired and injured to stay awake. Penelope insisted on taking a turn as well, and she was relieved when Wolf didn't fight her on it and let her join one of the pairs on their shift.

The MRE she'd had for dinner was one of the best things Penelope remembered eating in all of her life. Oh, it wasn't gourmet food by any stretch of the imagination, but having been deprived of real calories and a somewhat balanced meal for so long, it was heaven. She could only eat about half of everything because her stomach had shrunk so much during her captivity, but she swore she could feel her body literally absorbing the nutrients as she ate. She'd been given a canteen of her own, filled with the most beautiful, tasting water she'd ever had the privilege of drinking. Yeah, it had a metallic taste from the purification tablets that had been used to make sure it was safe, but Penelope wasn't going to complain.

Finally, after they'd been quiet for a while, Wolf asked what she'd been expecting him to bring up for most of the day.

"So, Tiger...can you tell us what the hell happened?

How did those bastards get their hands on you and the others?"

Penelope sighed. She didn't hesitate to tell the SEALs what happened. She'd waited a long time to tell someone, anyone, that she honestly didn't think it was their fault they were captured, that they weren't idiots who were running around the most dangerous section of the refugee camp as if they were at Disneyworld. "We were ordered to patrol the west side of the camp and look for trouble."

"By yourself? What idiot ordered that?" Dude asked immediately. After spending time in the camp looking for her, they obviously knew about the west side.

"Yeah. By ourselves. I protested the assignment as much as I could, but the major was new. New to the unit and new to combat. Granted, this wasn't really combat, but he had no idea how dangerous that side of the camp had gotten. The rest of us who had been there a while knew, and had been simply avoiding patrols over there. There really was no use. The thugs and terrorists had that side well and truly controlled, but the major decided that *he* knew best and our disagreeing was simply a matter of us being difficult. So we went."

Penelope shrugged and continued, "Thomas was the first to sense danger. We all knew we were closely watched while we patrolled, but he noticed that the same men watching us that day, had been following us the day before. While we'd been walking, they'd surrounded us, boxing us in. They had about twenty men to our four. We were sitting ducks. They beat the shit out of us and took our weapons. They dragged me off separately from the guys." Penelope tried to keep her voice emotionless and asked the question she already knew the answer to. "They're dead, aren't they?"

"Yeah," Dude confirmed.

Penelope didn't want to know any details, dead was dead, and continued on. "So they beat me up for a few days, then decided to throw me in front of the camera reading that asinine shit they called a manifesto or some such fucking thing. I did whatever they wanted and didn't put up a fight."

"Did they rape you?"

Cookie's words were pissed off and urgent…and to the point. Penelope figured there was some story there, but didn't ask and wasn't offended by the question. Hell, she was pretty surprised she hadn't been violated herself. "No. And before you ask, I'm not lying. They asked if I was a virgin, and I said no, which is the truth, by the way. I didn't want them trying to use me as a prize for some warped ideology they had. Of course, the suicide bomber is supposed to get the seventy-two virgins when they're *dead*, but I didn't want to risk someone trying to claim their virgin before they died."

"You know that's a myth right? Muslims don't really

believe that," Cookie told her matter-of-factly.

"I know, but I had no idea what *these* guys thought. We all know the sun rises in the east and sets in the west, but if someone is brainwashed enough they can swear in front of a judge that it's the opposite."

The men nodded in understanding.

"Were you held at the camp the entire time?" It was Mozart who asked.

"Yeah, I'm pretty sure. It was hard to tell because in the beginning, I was pretty out of it from the beatings, but after they stopped that shit, I don't think they moved me much."

"The pink material was genius, by the way," Wolf told her.

Penelope half laughed. "Well, I don't know about genius, but I figured it couldn't hurt. I never thought my fancy underwear would be strewn across a refugee camp when I put it on all those months ago. When they mummified me up every time I went outside the tent, I knew no one would be able to tell it was me, and that any clue I could drop would help someone find me if they were looking."

"How'd you know we'd be looking?"

"Well, I didn't, not for sure. But I know my brother. Cade wouldn't let me disappear without a trace."

"You'll be glad to know you're correct. He's been all over the news back home. Making petitions, organizing rallies, sending letters to the President, basically being a pest of the highest order," Benny told her.

"Great, I bet he even dragged out my stupid college graduation picture, didn't he?"

Wolf smiled. "Yeah, if it's the picture of you and him standing next to each other with his elbow resting on your head and you laughing hysterically."

Penelope laughed. "That's the one. I hate that picture, but he loves it. And the rest of it certainly sounds like him, and while I was being held captive, I counted on it. He's worked his ass off to get where he is today. He's one of the best firefighters San Antonio has ever seen."

"But you're not biased or anything," Benny joked.

"I'm not biased," Penelope said in a dead-even voice. "Yes, I'm related to him, but I've seen him in action," Penelope insisted and tried to explain. "Once, we arrived at a building fully engulfed in flames on the top three floors, but someone said there might be a child trapped inside. I know it's his job, but none of the other firefighters there would go in. Cade didn't even hesitate, but plunged right into the house and found her and brought her out alive."

"Sounds impulsive and risky to me," Dude commented dryly.

"From the outside looking in, it probably does, but he doesn't do anything impulsively. Not even close.

Cade knows fire. He knows how it behaves, and how it works. He's studied it and he has this weird sense for it. He told me afterwards that he could tell by the way it looked he knew he had time to get in, find the girl and get out. He's the least-impulsive man I've ever known in my life." Penelope knew her words were passionate, but she'd defend her brother to anyone, anytime. He was *that* good at what he did.

"Got anyone waiting for you back home?" Abe asked.

"Besides my family and fellow firefighters at Station 7 where I work? Nope. Between firefighting and the Army Reserves, I don't have a lot of extra time to date. Although after this, I think I'll be retiring from the Reserves. I'll be happy never to step foot outside Texas again."

Everyone chuckled lightly.

"What about you guys? I think you're all married, right? That's unusual for a SEAL team, isn't it?"

Wolf answered for the group. "Maybe. Being married to a SEAL isn't exactly a walk in the park. Our wives can't know where we're going or how long we'll be gone. Most can't handle the stress."

"But your wives can?" Penelope asked, genuinely curious.

"Yeah. Our wives can," Dude said firmly.

"That's great, really. Kids?"

"Yup. Abe's got two adopted daughters. They plucked them right out from under their worthless mother's nose and never looked back. Mozart has a six-month-old girl; Benny has two, a two-year-old daughter and a one-year-old son; and my wife is pregnant." Dude paused and laughed, but in a way Penelope could tell he wasn't amused. "Well, she was when I left. I was hoping to get home in time to see my daughter being born, but doesn't look like that's gonna happen now."

Penelope didn't know what to say. Sorry didn't seem to cut it, and besides, she wasn't the one who'd shot down their helicopter. Finally she said, somewhat lamely to her own ears, "They sound great."

"Yeah. They are great," Mozart agreed quietly.

The conversation seemed to dry up after that. Each lost in their own thoughts. Thinking about their loved ones and wondering when they'd get to see them again.

# Chapter Sixteen

FIONA PACED THE waiting room at the hospital. Because Faulkner wasn't available, Caroline was allowed to be in the delivery room with Cheyenne. They'd been there most of the day because no one wanted to take a chance on leaving and missing the birth of Cheyenne's baby. But after being cooped up all day, Jess had taken John and Sara out to get some fresh air, and Alabama had finally relented and taken Davisa and Brinique out to get something to eat. That left Summer with her infant daughter, Melody and Akilah, and Fiona...and Fiona couldn't sit still any longer.

Caroline had been periodically coming out with updates. Apparently the bleeding Cheyenne had at home when her water broke wasn't exactly serious, though the doctors were keeping their eye on it. But the women hadn't heard from Caroline in a while and Fiona was about to burst.

Just when Fiona didn't think she'd be able to stand it for a second longer, Caroline appeared in the doorway. She was as pale as the white tiles on the floor under their feet.

"Oh my God, is the baby okay? Cheyenne? What's wrong?" Fiona fretted, rushing over and grabbing Caroline's hands.

"The baby is perfect. Eight pounds, nine ounces—no wonder Shy looked like she was having triplets. Good lung sounds and all ten toes and fingers. Cutest little baby I've ever seen…including Jess's kids."

"Then what? What's wrong?" Fiona questioned.

"It's Cheyenne. She's bleeding and the doctors were having a hard time getting it stopped. They made me leave, but I heard the nurse tell the doctor she thought it was a postpartum hemorrhage."

Summer sucked in a sharp breath. "Oh my God, a hemorrhage? That doesn't sound good. Did they get it stopped?"

"I don't know. They kicked me out." Caroline took a deep breath, and when it came out, it was a sob. "She was s-s-so happy that the baby was fine, she'd b-b-been so worried. She held her in her arms and looked up at me and said she didn't feel so good. Then she went limp and just kinda faded away. I had to grab the baby so she didn't tumble out of Cheyenne's arms."

"Oh, Caroline, come 'ere." Fiona gathered Caroline in her arms and felt Melody crowd up against her back. Summer came up beside them and put one arm around

Caroline's shoulders and held baby April in the other. The four women stood in the busy waiting room in each other's arms, trying to take strength and comfort from one another. Fiona could feel Caroline shuddering against her and felt so helpless to do anything for her or for their friend.

Caroline finally got herself together and pulled back. "We were so worried about the baby, we didn't even *think* about anything happening to Cheyenne. She's too young for this."

"I don't think age has anything to do with it," Summer said gently. "Should we call the others?"

"I think Jess and Alabama will be back soon anyway, let's not freak them out until we have more information," Fiona said, not knowing if it was the right decision or not. "Maybe by the time they get back, the doctors will have come out here and told us she'll be fine."

"Come on, let's sit. There's nothing we can do but wait," Melody cajoled, and they all wandered over to a group of chairs in the corner of the room.

Twenty minutes later, Jessyka returned with her toddlers and ten minutes after that, Alabama came over with Davisa and Brinique in tow. It was a somber group that waited to hear from the doctor. They should've been thrilled beyond belief about the healthy newborn baby, but instead they were hoping they wouldn't have to get a Red Cross message to Commander Hurt and try to get Faulkner home to bury his wife.

Another hour passed before the group heard anything else about Cheyenne, and by that time everyone was more than ready to hear some news. The kids were restless and their grumpiness was making everyone edgy.

A nurse finally came into the waiting room and asked for Cheyenne's family. All six women got up and when the nurse saw how many of them there were, she led them all into a more private conference room. She stood looking at the large group of women and children as if she didn't know where to start.

"For God's sake, just tell us," Caroline pleaded, not able to stand the suspense any longer. "How's Cheyenne? When can we see her?"

"As you all know, there were…complications. Cheyenne was bleeding so heavily that she had to be transferred to the operating room."

"Oh. My. God," Melody whispered, saying out loud what everyone in the room was thinking. "Is she still alive?"

Everyone's eyes were glued to the harried-looking nurse sent into the lion's den, so to speak, to notify the family of the patient's condition.

"I understand her husband is in the service and is out of the country on a mission?" At the nods all around her, she said gravely, "I recommend he be contacted as soon as possible. He needs to get home. Now."

The waiting room was silent for a beat until Caroline's soft inhale and her devastated words as she repeated Melody's question. "Is Cheyenne still alive?"

# Chapter Seventeen

DUDE WOKE UP suddenly and lurched forward, choking back a cry. "Holy shit," he whispered into the chilly night air.

"You all right, Dude?" Wolf asked from beside him.

Dude ran his hand down his face and tried to clear the all too real images from his brain, and noticed his hand was shaking. His hand was fucking *shaking*. He was the unflappable one. The one who took things in stride. The Dom who was always in control. But at the moment he felt anything but strong. "No," he answered his friend.

"Wanna talk?"

No, Dude didn't want to talk, but he did anyway, thinking maybe it'd help him get back on track. "I dreamed Cheyenne had the baby."

"That's good, right?" Wolf asked, propping himself up on his uninjured elbow and keeping his voice quiet so he wouldn't disturb the others.

"Yeah, but right after she was born, Cheyenne

looked up at me, said she loved me and to make sure the baby knew how much she was loved by her mom, then closed her eyes and fucking died. Right there in front of me. I could hear our baby crying in the background and everything."

"It was just a dream, Dude. You're stressed about not being able to be there," Wolf said, trying to soothe his friend.

"Yeah, a dream. But it seemed too fucking real."

Wolf didn't know what to say to that. They both had seen some crazy shit in their lives, things some people would say were impossible. Because of that, they both knew that maybe Dude's dream wasn't so much a dream as it was foreshadowing. Finally, he told Dude in an earnest voice, "I'm doing everything I can to get us home."

"I know." Dude rubbed his hand down his face once more, feeling the beard that had grown in the weeks they'd been gone. Changing the subject, he asked, "How far north should we go?" Dude knew as well as Wolf that they needed to gain higher ground and find a good place to dig in and defend themselves. If push came to shove and they got into a firefight, they'd eventually lose, simply because they didn't have enough ammunition to outlast the insurgents. Their best bet was to hunker down and stay undetected long enough for Tex, and the government, to send in another chopper to get them the hell out of dodge.

"How far north?" Wolf repeated. "As far as we can. It's unlikely we can stay under their radar forever, especially since they could have thermal imaging and there are seven of us. If it was only one or two of us we could probably stay undetected, but we can't leave Benny and Abe alone, and I can't do much with this broken arm, so we have to stick together."

"As if we'd break up," Dude snorted.

Wolf smiled grimly. They both knew there was no way in hell they'd ever leave any of the others behind. They were too close to do that, and besides, they'd been trained way too well.

"What do you make of Tiger?" Dude asked. "Think she's telling the truth about not being violated?"

"Yeah, I do," Wolf said immediately, turning to look at the woman sleeping on the ground a bit away from them. They could hear her slightly snoring, but she was clearly out, sleeping the sleep of a woman who knows she's safe for the moment. "She's one tough cookie. I think she'd be more leery around us if she'd been raped."

"I agree to a point, but I also think she'd keep going until she fell over just so she wouldn't look weak in our eyes," Dude pointed out. "I've seen women like this before. They don't want to look weak in any way, so they'll lie and hide their pain, feelings, or thoughts, no matter how many times they're asked if they're okay."

Wolf knew Dude was talking about his experience as a Dominant, and he had a good point, but somehow Wolf knew in his gut, he was wrong this time. "Turner isn't the kind of soldier, or woman, to keep her thoughts inside. If she was upset, she wouldn't be afraid to let us know. Yesterday when she was hungry, she asked for something to eat. You told me yourself the first thing she did when you showed up in her tent, was ask for something to drink."

Dude nodded. "True."

Wolf continued, "She reminds me a lot of Caroline. She'll fight to the death to survive and to get respect. I think that's why she's so successful as a firefighter."

"Yeah."

"If you guys are done talking about me, can we get a move on or what?"

Dude and Wolf looked up in surprise, seeing Penelope was awake and leaning up on an elbow watching them.

"Yeah, as soon as we get the others up, we can finalize the plan for the day." Wolf didn't bother to apologize for talking about her. He smiled a bit at the scowl that moved across her face.

"Great," Penelope muttered and sat up, holding her ribs and groaning. She ignored her pain, as it was manageable, and moved over to Abe who was waking up as well. "How's the leg feel? Can I look at it?"

"Knock yourself out, Tiger." Abe's spoke quietly and if Penelope hadn't spent a lot of time taking care of injured people, she would've been fooled by his nonchalant tone of voice. He was in pain. A lot of it. She eased his ripped pants to the side and unwound the bandages she'd put on earlier. Penelope grimaced at the look of the wound.

"Fuck," Cookie said from behind her in a hushed voice.

Abe didn't pick his head up off the ground. "It's infected, isn't it?" he asked evenly.

"Yeah," Cookie agreed.

Penelope interrupted their monosyllable conversation. "Well, us swearing at it isn't going to magically make it any better. Cookie, think you can get me some more of those alcohol pads? And what kind of painkillers do we have? He needs something if we're going to get his ass up this mountain and to a safer place."

"Yes, ma'am," Cookie said with a smile on his face. There wasn't anything to smile about, but Penelope was so darn cute and feisty, he couldn't help it.

"I think—" Abe started, but Penelope interrupted him.

"No."

"No what?" Abe asked in confusion.

"No to whatever you were going to say. It was going

to be bullshit," Penelope told him without rancor, still concentrating on his leg.

Benny laughed from the sitting position he'd pulled himself into when he'd woken up. "She's got you pegged, Abe."

"Fuck off," Abe told his teammate and closed his eyes, but didn't resume saying whatever it was that had been on his mind.

Penelope smiled, enjoying the camaraderie of the men; it reminded her of the guys she worked with back in San Antonio. Taco and Driftwood were the comedians of the group, always ready with a quick comeback and joke. Chief was a lot like Wolf, in charge of them all, but also their friend too. Squirrel and Crash were like brothers to her, and of course Cade, otherwise known as Sledge, *was* her brother. Moose was quiet and introspective, but never missed anything going on around him. She missed them all fiercely, and would do whatever she could to get back to them and to hear their ribbing and joking around the station.

It was Wolf who handed her the alcohol pads from the first-aid kit. Penelope set to work trying to clean Abe's wound without hurting him too much, while Cookie injected more painkillers and antibiotics into his veins.

"Okay, we're going to continue to head up today, much as we did yesterday. We'll stop more often to drink and to check everyone's wounds. We need to be as close to one hundred percent as we can get if we're gonna make it out of here. Benny, you need to let us know if you continue to be dizzy or if you get nauseous. Dude, wrap your ankle up tight, but don't overdo it. When we stop, you need to put it up to try to keep the swelling down. Abe, talk to us about that leg. I don't want it falling off somewhere along the trail." The others chuckled at that, and Wolf continued, "Tiger, we'll wrap your ribs before we set out, but unfortunately there's not too much we can do about them. If you need something for the pain, let us know. You'll need to drink more than us as well, you have a lot of catching up to do. Also, make sure you continuously snack as the day goes on as well. You might be smaller than us, but you need the calories and energy."

Penelope nodded. Wolf was right, and he wasn't telling her anything she didn't already know she needed to do if she was going to be able to continue on and carry her own weight. Even though this was her rescue, she'd do whatever it took to not be a burden.

"I'll monitor my arm. It hurts, but it's not unbearable. You guys set it perfectly," Wolf complimented, looking at Penelope and Cookie. "We need to find a good hidey-hole today. If those bastards do have thermals, we'll need to be able to get far enough back and out of sight of anyone that might be scanning the area.

But at the same time, we need to be able to get out and to a rescue chopper at a moment's notice. Everyone keep your eyes open."

At the nods all around, the group got ready to head out. The day was going to be tough, but as every SEAL knew, the only easy day was yesterday.

# Chapter Eighteen

JESS AND SUMMER sat with their babies, and the others stood around the small conference room, waiting for the nurse to continue telling them what was going on with Cheyenne. Akilah was once again a lifesaver, taking over the entertainment of Sara.

"Cheyenne was transferred to the operating room as a precaution. Basically PPH is a condition where the uterus doesn't contract properly after giving birth. We gave her some painkillers and hand-delivered the placenta. Usually once the placenta is out, the uterus will start to contract on its own, and the bleeding will stop," the nurse explained slowly and carefully, looking at each woman to make sure they understood.

When everyone nodded, she continued. "We gave her some medicine to try to assist the uterus to contract, and thus stop the bleeding on its own, with no luck. The bleeding slowed, but didn't stop. Finally after a blood transfusion, and more specialized drugs, the bleeding stopped. We didn't have to do a hysterectomy, which was the next step if we couldn't get the bleeding stopped with these other measures."

"Oh my God, a hysterectomy," Jessyka breathed, putting a hand on her own still-flat stomach as if she could protect the baby growing there from the word.

"Yeah, but we didn't need to go that far. Cheyenne is fine for now. She's sleeping off the painkillers. I recommend getting her husband home as soon as possible because when she woke up, she was asking for him. She had a really close call today, and honestly, she's not completely out of the woods yet. She'll continue to get fluids and drugs to make sure her uterus stays contracted. She's going to need to stay here probably tonight and tomorrow night. After that, the doctor will take a look and see what she thinks about letting her go home. But once home, she'll need to take it easy and get lots of sleep, fluids, and good nutritious food. No fast food and no junk food for at least a couple of weeks. She'll need to rest and not overdo anything. It's been my experience that new moms want to get back into their normal routine as soon as possible, but that's not in her best interest. The doctor will prescribe some prenatal vitamins as well to make sure her folic acid and iron intake are high."

"Will she be able to breastfeed?" Summer asked.

"Of course. Nothing else about the care of her daughter will change." When everyone nodded in relief, the nurse continued. "If anyone has any other questions, don't hesitate to ask the nurse on duty on her floor. She's going to be in ICU tonight, and most likely in the morning she'll be moved to a regular floor. Only one of you will be able to see her tonight, but once she's completely awake and out of the woods, and she's moved to a regular room, you'll all be able to visit her…but I recommend not all at the same time."

This time the women in the room laughed lightly, relieved that it sounded like Cheyenne was going to be all right.

"Can we see baby?" Akilah asked.

The nurse turned to her and agreed. "Yes, but again, maybe take turns? There are a lot of you here."

"We will," Caroline reassured the friendly nurse. "Thank you for taking the time to talk to us and reassure us about Cheyenne. I'm not sure we can get her husband, or any of our husbands home right now, but we'll take care of her until he *can* get home. We'll take turns staying with her and browbeating her to take it easy. It's what we do best."

"You're more than welcome. And it's very nice to see that she's got such great friends. And by the way, thank you all for your husbands' service to our country. While they might be the ones doing the actual fighting, I know spouses also make a lot of sacrifices. So thank you."

The women all nodded their heads and watched as the nurse left the room. It was always nice to be included in the thanks, even if, as the nurse said, they weren't the ones out on the front lines.

"Caroline, you and Akilah and Melody go first to see Baby Cooper," Fiona said decisively. "We'll wait until you get back."

"Are you sure?" Caroline asked, looking around at the group of women in the room.

"Of course," Jessyka enthused. "We'll wait."

"Hey, Caroline, what did Cheyenne name the baby?" Alabama asked quietly.

"I don't know," Caroline answered. "She didn't have time before she passed out. The doctor had just put the baby in her arms and she was counting her fingers and toes when it happened."

Alabama laughed a little. "Figures. We'll just have to keep calling her Baby Cooper until Cheyenne can wake up and tell the doctor what to put on the birth certificate."

"Taylor!" Davisa said in the silence of the room.

"What, honey? Alabama asked her daughter.

"Taylor. It's the baby's name."

Alabama tried to let her new daughter down easily so she wasn't disappointed. "Davisa, that's a great name, but Cheyenne and Faulkner probably have a name in mind already."

"Taylor," the five-year-old insisted again stubbornly.

"We'll see," Alabama said, trying to head off a tantrum. All the other mothers in the room laughed, recognizing the avoidance technique.

"Okay, we'll be back. Alabama, Jess, and Summer, you guys need to get your kids home and to bed. We'll be quick and you can take your turn. Fiona and I will stay the night and the rest of you can come back tomorrow," Caroline said, trying to organize the group.

"I stay too," Akilah insisted.

Caroline looked at Melody, who was looking at her daughter, deciding whether or not they should stay. Finally she nodded. "Yeah, we'll stay with you guys too."

"Okay, it's a plan. We'll hurry and you guys can see the new baby and get out of here."

Everyone agreed and the trio headed out of the conference room and continued toward the viewing room where the babies were kept while waiting to go home with their new moms and dads.

When they were on their way, Caroline asked Melody quietly, "Are you going to call Tex? I can call the commander if you take care of Tex."

Melody nodded. "Yeah, I'll do it as soon as we see Cheyenne's baby." They both knew Tex would do what he could to get word to the team about Cheyenne's condition and the birth of Faulkner's daughter. Melody remembered the news story about the crashed helicopter, and decided once again to keep it to herself. This was no time to bring it up, and besides, it might not be at all relevant anyway.

# Chapter Nineteen

PENELOPE LOOKED AROUND the cave with a critical eye. It wasn't huge, but it was big enough for all seven of them to fit inside comfortably. Cookie and Mozart had been mostly carrying Abe by the time they'd come up on the hole in the side of the mountain. Wolf was the one who spotted the cave first.

It was about halfway up a steep, rocky incline and the opening was only partly visible from where they'd been hiking. Cookie, Mozart, and Wolf had headed up the uneven terrain to check it out. They'd returned thirty minutes later with the news that they thought it would work.

Penelope felt bad for Cookie and Mozart, as they ended up making *three* trips up the mountainside, helping their teammates hoof it to their new hidey-hole.

There were some scrub bushes growing alongside the opening, giving them a place to take care of personal business. There was no clear or easy way to continue up the side of the mountain if they needed to make a quick exit, but there were a lot more of the scrub bushes that could give some cover if they needed it.

Penelope didn't want to ask, but she couldn't help it. She was never one to hold back when she had questions, so she didn't even try. "What now?"

"What now?" Mozart repeated.

"Yeah, what now? We're sitting tight in this hole in a rock, but for how long? What's the plan?"

"The plan is to wait," Wolf answered calmly.

"Wait?" Penelope asked incredulously. "For what?"

"Tex."

Penelope massaged her temples. "Who the fuck is Tex? That's like the third time you've mentioned him. And you should all know, I'm not good at waiting."

None of the men tensed up, none of them looked upset in any way. It was Cookie who answered, but not in the way Penelope would've thought. "About two and a half years or so ago, we were in Mexico on a rescue mission. We were sent in to rescue a young woman who'd been kidnapped. When we got there, we found another woman who had also been kidnapped, but no one was looking for her. We ended up all getting out of the country without any injuries."

He paused, and that gave Penelope enough time to ask, "I don't understand what—"

"Listen, Tiger," Wolf scolded.

Penelope shut her mouth and nodded, holding back

her frustration at the cryptic answer to her question.

"Fiona seemed to be all right on the outside. She was brave and stoic, much as you are, Penelope. She'd been drugged and fought the addiction and came through the other side. I didn't follow my instincts and thought she was good. We left on a mission and Fee had a flashback. She thought she was back in Mexico and she ran. Ran from phantom kidnappers who only existed in her mind. I was out of the country and couldn't get back home for at least a day and a half. In the meantime, she was out there, alone, freaked-out, and suffering."

Cookie took a deep breath, then continued, "Tex found her. He tracked her down and kept her safe until I could get home. I trust Tex with my life, with my wife's life, with my teammates' lives and with their women's lives. Tex will find us. I'd stake everything I own, including my life, on it."

"You *are* staking your life on it," Penelope murmured, still not one hundred percent sure they should put all their proverbial eggs into Tex's basket.

"Tiger, each of us sitting here today owes everything to Tex. He's been responsible in some way for helping each of us save the lives of our wives. I can guarantee that right this moment he's doing everything he can to bring us home," Benny said seriously.

Penelope looked at the SEAL who so far had been

the quietest as he continued speaking.

"We don't ask, he doesn't tell, but we all know what he does isn't quite legal, but none of us give a fuck. He knows people. He used to be a SEAL himself, but he works with the CIA, FBI, Delta Force, the Rangers, and I wouldn't be surprised if he didn't personally know some fucking terrorist over here in Iraq who owes him a favor. If he has to, Tex will mobilize every single one of them to get us the fuck out of here. You just have to have faith."

"It's not in me to trust," Penelope said honestly, "but I trust *you* guys. You got me out of that hellhole I was being held in. If you say I should trust this Tex person, I will."

"Good," Benny nodded in satisfaction.

"But…"

All six men groaned and Penelope couldn't help but smile. They were all such…guys, it wasn't funny. "Do we have a plan for what we're gonna do if the insurgents find us before Tex gets the cavalry here?"

"Yeah. Stay alive."

Penelope growled in frustration at Abe's response. She shook her head. "Never mind. Jesus."

Wolf spoke up again. "We've all got ammo and weapons, Tiger. We'll fight whoever dares show their face near this hole. We aren't just gonna sit here and let someone kill us."

"What if they use an RPG?" Penelope asked, voicing one of her greatest fears.

"They might."

Penelope wasn't reassured by Wolf's comment, but he continued before she could say anything.

"But it's a chance we're going to have to take. We'll hang low until we absolutely have to engage them in battle. If luck is with us, the worst they have is grenades."

"Shit," Penelope whispered, horrified, imagining one of the insidious little devices being lobbed into the cave and blowing up, killing them all.

"Fuck," Dude said under his breath. "Way to freak her out, Wolf."

"Look," Wolf cautioned, "There's no guarantee we'll come out of this alive, but if you follow our lead, we'll get you out, we *have* had experience in this shit."

Penelope thought about it and decided to let it go. Wolf was right. She was grilling them over something they couldn't possibly predict. They were trained SEALs. When put into a dangerous situation, they acted, just as she did when she was thrust into a situation inside a burning building. If they were civilians inside a burning building, would she want them asking as many questions as she had been of these men? No. It would just piss her off. She'd tell them to trust her and follow her lead.

She took a deep breath and said, "You're right. I'll do whatever you tell me to do if the shit hits the fan. Promise."

Wolf nodded in relief. "Good."

An uneasy silence fell over the group as they all waited for something…anything…to happen.

TEX CONCENTRATED ON the computer screen in front of him. He'd worked with Keane "Ghost" Bryson on a mission in the past. The Delta Force soldier was damn good at his job and had actually saved Tex's life. They hadn't talked in person after that mission, but they had kept in touch periodically over the years electronically.

Commander Hurt already had intel that the helicopter had crashed, but hadn't known where. Tex passed along the coordinates and knew the SEAL team that was already in the country was being mobilized, but Tex had a gut feeling his friends were going to need additional backup.

It seemed obvious that Wolf and his team had left four trackers with four people who were either injured or dead, and had kept the last one for themselves. There was no way they'd split up otherwise. Tex watched as the single red dot made its way north, away from the others. The question was, who was with each of the trackers.

If Wolf needed additional backup, that's exactly what he was going to do his best to send to them. The SEALs couldn't have crashed in a worse place. They'd landed smack-dab in the middle of Insurgent Central. It was as if they'd been plunked down on top of a hornets' nest…and slowly but surely the hornets were swarming out of that nest looking for what had disturbed them.

But that's where Ghost and his Delta Force team came in. Tex contacted Ghost as soon as he hung up with the commander. He'd listened to Tex's concerns and immediately got in touch with *his* commander. The government typically didn't work that quickly, but Ghost and his Delta Force team obviously had a lot of pull and within a few hours, the Deltas were on their way to the Middle East.

Tex kept his eyes on the screen. On the left side there were four motionless blinking red dots and one lone red dot getting further and further away from the others. On the right side of the screen was a satellite picture. A surprisingly crisp and clear picture. Tex had hacked into the government's top-secret satellites and was looking at a live feed over the mountains of Turkey. He looked on, helpless, as shadowy figures moved closer and closer to the four unmoving dots hidden on the hillside.

He held his breath in frustration, knowing all he could do was watch.

# Chapter Twenty

*It's been two days since reports of a helicopter crashing in the mountains between Turkey and Iraq. There hasn't been any confirmation of who was onboard that helicopter or of any casualties as a result of the crash. The President has been close-lipped about the incident and, unusually, there have been no leaked reports of any kind.*

*No terrorist group has claimed responsibility for the crash yet, and even ISIS has been silent.*

*You might remember that Sergeant Penelope Turner was kidnapped by ISIS terrorists and has been seen fairly regularly in propaganda videos. News of Sergeant Turner's fate is still unknown as of now, but there's speculation of a connection between the helicopter crash and Sergeant Turner.*

*Stay tuned for our report at ten, where we delve deeper into the life of a Navy SEAL and what goes into preparing for a rescue attempt. We will be interviewing a retired member of SEAL Team Six, which, as you know, was one of the main forces behind the mission that finally killed Osama Bin Laden in 2011.*

CHEYENNE LOOKED UP at one of her best friends as she held her new baby in her arms and said, "I dreamed I was lying in bed and I looked up at Faulkner, told him I loved him and to make sure our baby knew how much I loved her. Then I closed my eyes and died."

Jessyka sat next to Cheyenne's bed and squeezed her free hand tightly. "But you're here now."

Cheyenne nodded, but didn't say anything for a long while. She simply looked down at her daughter lovingly.

Jess finally broke the silence. "So…are you going to put us out of our misery and tell us what you named your beautiful daughter?"

Jess was horrified to see tears rise in Cheyenne's eyes and roll down her face.

"Oh my God, what is it? What'd I say?" Jess asked frantically, concerned she'd said something to upset her friend.

Cheyenne looked up at Jess again. "It's s-stupid. I just…I just thought I'd be sitting here with Faulkner. That we'd greet our baby together, we'd fill out her birth certificate together."

Jess leaned over and held Cheyenne as best she could

with the baby between them. She whispered in her ear as she held her friend, "Seriously, I *know*. But he'll be home soon and you'll have a ton of other memories to make together. It sucks that he's not here, but think about how you now get to hand her to him when he *does* get home and introduce him to his daughter for the first time. It's not the same, but it'll be special in its own way."

Jess felt Cheyenne nod against her and sniff once. She pulled back and reached over for a tissue. She wiped Cheyenne's tears from her face and then handed it over so she could blow her nose. Once her friend had gotten control over her emotions, Jess asked again, "So…you gonna tell me her name, or keep it a secret forever and make me call your daughter 'girl' for the rest of her life?"

Cheyenne smiled, as she knew Jess had planned for her to. "Taylor Caroline Cooper."

Jess looked startled for a moment, then beamed. "Holy crap. Davisa told me that's what you were going to call her, but I didn't believe her. Have you told Caroline yet?"

"That kid is smart, and no, I haven't told Caroline yet."

"Promise I can be there when you do."

Cheyenne laughed softly. "Promise."

Jess hugged her friend one more time, then stood up. "Okay, I have to get back to my monsters now, but we'll all be back this afternoon to take both of you to Caroline's house."

"Oh, but I thought—"

"Nope," Jess interrupted. "I know you thought you were going home, but you aren't. The doctor said you needed to take it easy and we all know if we let you go home, you won't. And until Faulkner is back, we're going to make sure you follow the doc's instructions to a tee."

"I won't—"

Jess interrupted again, "Yes, you would. But now you won't."

Cheyenne sighed in mock agitation and huffed, "Fi-ne."

"Fine." Jess smiled. "So as I was saying, we'll be back this afternoon to bring you home to Caroline's. Be good and I'll see you in a bit. I've called the nurse and she's gonna come and get Taylor. You need some rest before we spring you from here."

"Okay. Thanks, Jess."

"No thanks necessary. You scared the hell out of us. We're just glad you're all right, and we're planning on making sure you stay that way."

"You're acting as bossy as Faulkner."

"Ha, as if," Jess snorted. "That man has cornered the market on bossy...and you love it."

"I do. Any word?"

Jess knew what Cheyenne meant. "No. Nothing."

"Did you ask Melody?"

Jess shook her head. "No. I don't really want to pressure her about it. I don't want her to feel like she's a middle-man between us and what Tex knows."

Cheyenne nodded. "Yeah, it's not fair of us to ask, is it?"

"Not really, but I'm sure she'd tell us if she knew anything."

"Hummmm." Cheyenne didn't agree or disagree with Jess. She'd only seen Melody once since she'd woken up in the hospital, but the worried lines around her mouth and the smile that didn't seem to be as honest as usual made her think Melody knew more than she was saying. But she let it go. "Thanks for everything. I'll see you later."

Jess nodded and left, smiling at the nurse who was arriving to take little Taylor back to the nursery.

MELODY SAT IN the room Caroline and Wolf had set up like a little apartment in the basement of their house with her back against the wall and her knees bent up with her arms around them. There was a perfectly good bed and chair she could've sat on, but for some reason she felt more comfortable curled up where she was. Melody held the phone up to her ear, fingers white against the plastic.

"You haven't heard from them?" she asked Tex, voice wobbling.

"No."

Melody knew Tex was deliberately being vague, but his vagueness wasn't reassuring her at all. "Do you think they're alive?"

"Yes."

"How do you know if you haven't heard from them?"

"Mel," Tex's voice was quiet and reassuring, "they might be your friends' husbands, and you might know them as those kids' fathers who go ga-ga over every little move they make, but I know them as lethal, bad-ass Navy SEALs."

Melody could read between Tex's words. "Right."

"I love you, baby. Don't worry about this. Well, as much as possible. I honestly don't know what's going on, but rest assured I'm doing everything in my power to get them home. Okay?"

"Okay, Tex."

"Now, how's my girl?"

Melody smiled, loving how much Tex loved Akilah. "She's good. I've been helping her with her prosthetic every night, even though she really doesn't need my help much anymore. She's been great with Jess's kids and little Sara has really taken to her."

"Yeah?"

"Yeah."

Tex was silent a moment, then said, "I've been thinking about it. We talked about it before Akilah came into our lives, but we haven't had a chance since then. But I want a baby with you, Melody. I want a daughter with your blonde hair, your beautiful eyes and features running around. I'd love to give Akilah a little sister of her own."

When Melody didn't say anything, Tex asked worriedly, "Mel?" Then he heard a sniff. Oh shit. "Mel? I'm sorry, I didn't mean to make you cry."

"Did you mean it?"

"Every last word."

"I want that too," Melody breathed, wiping away the tears from her face.

"Thank fuck," Tex said under his breath. "When are you coming home?"

"Cheyenne comes home from the hospital today. We were going to go and stay with Jess to help her with John and Sara. I didn't really have a date in mind, but now I want to come home tomorrow."

Tex chuckled. "There's no rush, Mel. You need to go off the pill, and it could take a while for you to get pregnant anyway."

"I know, but that doesn't mean that I don't want to enjoy the process."

"Jesus, Mel. Seriously…you can't do this to me."

Melody giggled. "Okay, sorry. How about this. I'll stay for another week. That'll give you time to hopefully get the guys home, we'll be able to help Jess and spend time with the rest of the girls."

"Sounds good."

"Okay, but Tex…"

"Yeah, baby?"

"Think Amy will look after Akilah for a weekend when we get home? I'd like to give the baby-making thing my best shot, and that's easier if our daughter isn't in the next room."

"I'll call her as soon as we hang up, but consider it done. Amy's your best friend, she'd do anything for you. Fuck, I love you, Mel."

Melody smiled and hugged her knees harder. "And I love you too. Kiss Baby for me."

"I will. She's been whining at the front door every night. She obviously misses you." Tex's voice turned serious. "Stay strong, Mel. Those men are coming home sooner rather than later if I have anything to say about it."

"I know. You're Super Tex. You'll do your thing."

"Text me to let me know what you're up to."

"I will. Love you, Tex."

"Love you to Vegas and back. Stay safe."

"Bye."

"Bye."

Melody clicked off the phone and put her head on her knees. So many emotions were coursing through her brain, she didn't know which to process first. Worry for her friends, satisfaction that Akilah was settling in, happiness that Cheyenne was going to be okay and had a healthy new baby, love for her husband, *lust* for her husband, and a deep-seated contentment that Tex wanted a baby with her.

She sighed and finally stood up. It was time to go get Cheyenne and her newborn and get them settled.

# Chapter Twenty-One

THE ECHO OF a gunshot startled Penelope and she sat upright in confusion. Looking around, she saw Dude and Cookie lying on their stomachs at the front of the cave. Mozart and Benny were nowhere to be seen. Wolf was standing at the side of the cave, his pistol in his hand by his side. Every now and then he'd lean and peek out, then bring his head back inside.

Abe lay still and quiet behind her. He hadn't gotten any better, no matter how many antibiotics they'd pumped into him. His leg needed more attention than they could give him in the field. Penelope worried that if they didn't get him real medical care, at the very least, he could lose his leg, at worst…his life.

More shots rang out and Penelope flinched again, but forced herself to crawl over to Wolf's side. "What's up?" she whispered, feeling stupid for trying to be quiet, but not able to help herself. They were hiding, it seemed like the right thing to do, but there was no way anyone would be able to hear her with the distance the gunshots were from their location.

"Gunshots." Wolf's answer was short and succinct.

"No shit, Sherlock," was Penelope's irritated response. When no one laughed, she got serious. "Are they shooting at us?"

"No."

Penelope sighed. Getting information out of these men was like pulling teeth. She lay on her stomach, ignoring the twinges from her ribs, and crawled over to Dude and Cookie. She peered out of the cave and saw nothing. "Who are they shooting at?"

"Don't know."

"Is that good or bad?" Penelope asked.

"Could go either way," Dude told her.

"So what're we doing?"

"Waiting," Cookie answered.

"Waiting sucks," Penelope murmured, backing away from the front of the cave and heading back over to Abe. She wanted to take another look at his leg. She'd clean it again, hopefully that would help in some way.

GHOST HELD UP his hand to signal his team to stop. They'd HALO'd into the country and made their way toward the coordinates Tex had sent to them. Ghost respected the hell out of Tex. He was someone who Ghost was happy to know. He was a man who knew how to get things done. And if Tex wanted a favor, Ghost and the rest of his team were more than happy to grant it. Lord knew he'd helped them out more than once.

Fletch and Coach fanned out to his right and Hollywood and Beatle came up on his left flank. Ghost knew Blade and Truck were protecting their rear. He crouched down and waited for the insurgents to show themselves. None of them figured they'd be able to march right up to where Tex said there should be at least four men without running into trouble. Soon enough, that trouble made itself known.

The warning came through his earpiece just as the first gunshot rang out through the mountainside. The Delta Force team quickly made their way toward the firefight, adrenaline coursing through their blood, ready for a fight.

The sound of gunfire was sporadic and loud as it echoed through the hills. Instead of rushing in with guns blazing, Ghost and his team operated like the apparition their leader was named for. Four terrorists were dead before they'd even comprehended someone was behind them. Ghost motioned for Fletch and Beatle to make their way west, and he, Coach, and Blade made their way east. Truck and Hollywood quietly headed up toward where they hoped they'd find the missing SEALs.

The operatives made short work of the remaining terrorists in the area, knowing full well more were probably on their way as they headed up to meet their teammates.

"Five to one," Ghost heard in his ear.

"One, this is five, go ahead," he responded.

"All clear to approach."

"Clear." Ghost knew the other men heard the exchange and they carefully made their way up to where the SEALs were supposed to be. They arrived to find four men, not six, and no kidnapped Army sergeant to be seen.

They were surprised to realize it was the Night Stalker crew of the helicopter. The copilot and the gunner were deceased. The pilot and crew chief were alive, but in bad shape. They'd been the ones shooting back at the terrorists and defending their position.

Ghost crouched down next to the pilot and watched as Truck checked him over and started first aid on him. He looked over to the crew chief and watched as Beatle did what he could to make that man comfortable. "Sit rep?" he asked the pilot.

"Eleven on board. RPG came out of nowhere and we went down. Copilot was killed in the crash."

"Status of the others?"

"Honestly, I'm not sure," the pilot told Ghost in a dim, pained voice. "I was mostly out of it. They spoke to us before they left, but not what their plan was. Some of them were injured."

"The female?"

"Safe, Sir."

Something loosened inside Ghost knowing that Sergeant Turner had apparently been rescued, but he didn't let on. "They left you here?" His words were obviously not as toneless and emotionless as he wanted them to be when the pilot hurried to reassure him.

"Yes, but not like you might be thinking. They told me about the trackers they were leaving with us and made sure we knew the odds. We encouraged them to go. If they tried to take us with them, all of our chances would have been shit."

Ghost nodded. He didn't want to think badly of the SEALs. Thank God they were operating all on the same page. "Did they say where they were going?"

"Nothing other than up. They wanted to take a defensible position against the insurgents and figured their best chance would be up in one of the caves. They also hoped their moving would lead the terrorists away from us."

Ghost nodded, knowing it was what he would've done if he was in their position too. He thought quickly about their next plan of action. He wasn't going to leave these men here, not if he could help it.

He stood and headed off to the side and motioned

for his men to follow. They gathered together out of hearing of the injured Night Stalkers.

He did what he always did, laid out their options so they could decide as a team their next steps. "One, we leave the Night Stalkers here and head up to find the SEALs and our sergeant. Two, we take the Night Stalkers with us and head up to find the SEALs and our sergeant. Three, we call in for a helo to pick up the Night Stalkers and after they're up and away, we continue north to the SEALs and our sergeant. Four, we split up and three of us stay here with the Night Stalkers, and the rest of us head north. When we find the SEALs, we head back down here then call for pickup."

Ghost's men answered immediately with exactly the option he figured they would.

"Three," Hollywood said.

"Three," Beatle confirmed.

"Three," Blade also agreed.

The others chimed in with their agreement as well and everyone chose option three, without hesitation. There was no way they'd leave their comrades behind for the terrorists to get their hands on. Delta Force teams were under the umbrella of the U.S. Army, but all Special Forces teams were all brothers at heart.

The SEAL team planting mysterious trackers on the injured Army crew saved at least two men's lives. Ghost knew he'd be having a conversation with Tex about the trackers, and what the fuck an elite Navy SEAL team was doing wearing them on a top-secret mission. It was obviously not sanctioned by anyone at JSOC or the Navy, but at the moment he was damn glad for them.

Ghost nodded at his team, knowing they'd made the right decision, and reached for his radio. The right decision wasn't necessarily the safest decision, but they'd deal with any fallout as it came.

Two hours and two skirmishes with insurgents later, an MH-60 came screaming over the nearest hill toward them. If Ghost hadn't been used to it, it would've scared the shit out of him. Fletch and Coach grabbed the two deceased men, and Hollywood and Truck helped the two injured men into the helicopter. They'd barely handed the soldiers into the arms of the men waiting inside the chopper when it took off back the way it came. The entire rescue operation took about two-point-five minutes.

When the sound of the helicopter faded into the mountains, Ghost looked at his team. "Playtime's over. Let's go get our soldier back."

The others nodded, faces determined. It wouldn't matter how many terrorists got in their way. It was time to bring Sergeant Penelope Turner home.

# Chapter Twenty-Two

*Reports have come in about the helicopter crash we reported on last night in the mountains between Turkey and Iraq. A confidential source has reported to us that there were four men brought to Ramstein Air Base in Germany, two deceased and two injured. We have not been able to confirm their identities, but our source says they were in the helicopter when it crashed. There's no word on whether any of the four people were female. We will continue to try to get more information and to see if Sergeant Penelope Turner was among the wounded or deceased who were aboard the helicopter when it went down. Tune in later tonight.*

CAROLINE STOOD IN front of the small television in her and Matthew's bedroom and gasped after hearing the newscaster's latest story. It didn't say a lot, but it said enough. Helicopter crash. Two men dead, two men hurt, not a lot of information. Of course, there were six on Wolf's team, but the news could've gotten their information wrong.

She could feel her heart beating way too hard, but no tears would come. She stood staring at the TV, even though there was a silly ad on. Caroline wasn't seeing it, she was lost in her own worry and fear for her husband and her friends' husbands.

"Hey, Caroline, where can I find… Caroline?" Melody's words tapered off when she saw her friend standing in the middle of her bedroom, arms around her waist, whimpering softly. Melody went to her and put one arm around her, and put a hand lightly on Caroline's cheek and turned her face so she could see it clearly. "What is it, Caroline?" Melody whispered.

She watched as Caroline blinked once, then twice, before literally pulling herself together in front of Melody's eyes. "What? Um…"

Melody let go of Caroline's face, but turned to the TV as the news came back on. Suddenly realizing what might have been wrong, Melody asked carefully, "Did they have a report on the helicopter crash in the Middle East?"

At her words, Caroline turned suddenly and looked her in the eyes. "Yes."

"What'd they say?" Melody said softly.

"Two injured, two dead. They brought them to Ramstein Air Base in Germany."

"Any other information?"

"No."

Melody paused. "I don't have any information, Caroline, but for what it's worth, Tex thinks they're coming home."

Both women knew they were skirting the edge of what they promised they'd never do, speculate about their men's missions, but realizing they each knew more than they'd admitted up until now was a relief.

"It's worth a lot," Caroline told her. They hugged each other tightly and didn't let go until they heard a knock on the door. It was Akilah.

"Did you find paper plates?"

Caroline pulled back and looked at Melody questioningly.

Melody shrugged. "I came up to ask if you had any and where they might be. We thought it'd be better to serve everyone on the paper plates so we wouldn't have to do dishes later."

"Good thinking. And yes, I have some. I'll come down and show you where they are."

Melody nodded and she and Caroline linked elbows and headed out of the room and downstairs. Everyone was coming over to Caroline's and would be there in about an hour. They were serving all finger foods and celebrating Cheyenne's continued improvement and her new daughter. Cheyenne promised she'd reveal the name of her daughter that night as well.

She'd been as cagey as Kason was with his nickname and refused to tell them what she'd named her baby, saying she wanted to wait until they were all together. Caroline had rolled her eyes, but honestly didn't care. Cheyenne was alive and healthy, so she'd wait until she was ready to tell them all.

Caroline was thankful for Melody's help with the get-together. Seven adults, two kids, one near-teenager, two toddlers and a newborn were a bit daunting, even for Caroline.

Melody, Caroline, and Akilah worked alongside each other to put together various appetizers, a veggie tray, deviled eggs, and little peanut butter sandwiches for the kids. Cheyenne sat in the nearby family room, dozing before everyone arrived.

Finally when the food and drinks were almost ready, the other women started arriving. After all the greetings and cooing over Cheyenne's baby was done, everyone scattered around Caroline's living room. It was a tight fit, but they'd pushed the coffee table out of the way and brought up two chairs from the basement.

Cheyenne was in the big, fluffy armchair, holding her sleeping daughter in her arms. Jess, Summer, and Fiona were sitting on the large dark-brown leather couch, Alabama was in the other armchair, and Caroline and Melody were flitting back and forth to the kitchen, refilling drinks and bringing in more food for everyone when they ran out. They finally settled on the floor in front of the couch. Akilah was sitting next to Sara in front of all of them, playing with her quietly. John had finally crashed after running rampant throughout the house on his wobbly one-year-old legs. And even Brinique and Davisa had settled down and seemed content to be playing with some ancient dolls Caroline had unearthed from somewhere.

The room was full of love and contentment and Caroline was overjoyed to be a part of it. She thanked her lucky stars, as well as fate, every day that she'd been seated next to Matthew on that flight so long ago.

"All right, Cheyenne. Spill," Alabama griped good-naturedly at their friend. "I swear if you think you're gonna pull a Benny with us we might have to use drastic tickling measures to get it out of you. What is your beauty's name?"

Cheyenne didn't hesitate and smiled broadly as she announced, "Taylor Caroline Cooper."

Everyone oohed and ahhed and got up to step closer to Cheyenne and Taylor to congratulate her…again. Everyone except for Caroline.

Davisa watched as Caroline slipped out of the room and into the kitchen. She was confused. She thought her new mom's friend would've been happy to have the new baby named after her. She gave the doll she'd been playing with to Brinique, and followed Caroline.

She found her in the kitchen. Caroline was leaning against the counter with tears coursing down her face. "You aren't happy?" Davisa asked.

Caroline jerked in surprise, not having heard anyone come in after her. She turned and looked at Alabama's daughter. Her brow was furrowed and she looked terribly concerned…for her. Caroline wiped the tears from her face and tried to get control of herself. "I'm happy."

"Why are you crying then?"

"Sometimes people cry when they're happy, Davisa. I was surprised Cheyenne gave her daughter my name."

"They decided on that name a long time ago."

"What?" Caroline asked in surprise.

"Yeah, I heard her and Uncle Dude talking one night when they were looking after me and Brinique. They were laughing and giggling about first names, but Caroline was the first name they agreed on for her middle name."

Caroline could feel the tears welling up again. Well shit. Davisa continued.

"Uncle Dude's favorite name out of all of the names they talked about was Taylor, so I thought that was what Cheyenne would pick."

"You're a smart little girl. Did you know that?" Caroline asked, once again wiping away her tears.

"Yeah. I know."

Caroline smiled. "Come on, let's go back in and see little Taylor Caroline…shall we?"

"Okay, but I don't like babies. I'll wait until she's older then we can play Barbies together."

Caroline didn't have the heart to tell Davisa that by the time Taylor was old enough to want to play with Barbies, Davisa would probably be too old and would've moved on to other things. She took her hand and they walked back into the family room. She saw Cheyenne look up in concern and Caroline went right to her, letting go of Davisa's hand and watching her go back over to her sister and the pile of Barbie dolls.

Cheyenne grabbed Caroline's hand as she got close and Caroline sat down at the edge of the chair.

"Taylor is beautiful. I've never been so honored in all my life."

"Faulkner and I talked about it a lot. He has the utmost respect for Matthew, both as a man and as his team leader. If this baby was a boy, he would've had the middle name Matthew, but we figured we could just as easily honor the two of you by giving her your name as the middle name. It was the easiest part of naming this child, to tell you the truth."

Caroline felt her lip quivering again, and waited until the need to burst into noisy, messy tears passed before speaking. "I don't know how we all got so lucky, but thank God we all found each other." There was so much more she wanted to say, but Taylor chose that moment to wake up and she let out a screech. That in turn woke up April, who added her cries to the commotion.

The women and children spent another few hours together, laughing and smiling with each other. Finally, when the kids started getting grumpy and sleepy, everyone packed up to go to their own homes.

Melody was leaving with Jessyka to help her out for a few days before heading home to Virginia. Alabama got her girls ready to go, including the entire box of Barbies that Caroline said they could use until they decided they wanted to play with something else. Fiona helped Summer gather up her things, and finally Caroline and Cheyenne were left alone.

The house was quiet again at last.

"As much as I love everyone, I have to admit I love the peace and quiet that is left when they're all gone."

Cheyenne chuckled softly, making sure not to wake up Taylor, who was sleeping peacefully in a portable crib next to her chair. "Yeah, I have a feeling I'll be one of the people you'll be glad to see the back of in a few months when Taylor gets a bit older and more demanding."

The two friends smiled at each other. "You ready for bed?" Caroline asked.

Cheyenne smothered a yawn. "Yeah, I think so. Is it

sad that I'm excited about going to bed every night?"

"No, you've had a tough few days. Give your body time to heal. Don't be so hard on yourself."

"Have I thanked you for everything you've done for me, Caroline?"

"Yes, but you know I'd do anything for you."

"Well, you being there when Faulkner couldn't meant the world to me, and him. He'd say the same thing if he was here."

"They'll be home soon, I feel it."

"I hope so."

"Believe it." Caroline helped Cheyenne up and out of the chair and lifted Taylor into her arms as they headed down the stairs to the basement. "You've got the walkie-talkie so you can call me in the night if you need help, right?" Caroline asked bossily.

"Yes, ma'am."

Caroline sighed. "You won't call me, will you?"

"No. But I'll be fine. Swear."

"Okay, but please know I'm here if you need me."

"I do know it. And appreciate it."

Caroline put Taylor into her crib next to the bed and watched as the baby shifted and then settled into a deep sleep again. She leaned over and hugged Cheyenne. "Thank you for honoring me as you did. I love you, woman."

Cheyenne hugged Caroline back. "Love you too."

Caroline left her friend and headed up the stairs. She closed the basement door and made sure all the doors to the house were locked. She checked the kitchen and started the dishwasher. They didn't have many things to wash, only some platters and cups, but Caroline wanted to get the washing out of the way before she went to bed.

She turned off the lights, except for one in the kitchen, in case Cheyenne needed something in the middle of the night, and finally headed upstairs to her and Matthew's bedroom. She got ready for bed and slipped on a T-shirt of Matthew's. She crawled under the covers and pulled the pillow Matthew usually used into her body and cuddled it close. It didn't smell like him anymore, he'd been gone too long.

After everything that had happened that day, Caroline finally let go enough to let herself cry. And it wasn't a dainty cry. It was a gut-wrenching, I-miss-my-man, hope-he-is-safe-and-uninjured-and will-be-home-soon cry.

Caroline fell asleep with tears on her face and Matthew's face imprinted on her mind.

# Chapter Twenty-Three

WOLF AND HIS teammates stayed alert throughout the night and into the next morning. They heard gunshots every now and then, but hadn't seen any people. Wolf and Cookie looked at each other as they heard the telltale sound of an MH-60. They waited and watched, but never caught sight of it.

They knew Penelope hadn't even heard it, or if she did, she never commented on it. The chopper was there one minute and gone the next. Wolf hoped like hell they'd gotten there in time to rescue the Night Stalkers. He didn't regret his decision to leave them, but it still ate at him like an ulcer. They weren't used to leaving anyone behind, so the thought that perhaps, just perhaps, Tex had come through and gotten a rescue put into place to come retrieve their fellow military comrades, felt good.

Now the question was…who was coming for them, and when? And Wolf had no doubt someone *was* coming for them. No doubts whatsoever.

"Wolf, ten o'clock." Cookie's voice was low and urgent.

Wolf looked to where Cookie indicated and saw movement. He took out his binoculars and scanned the area below them. "I see them. Also nine, three, and twelve." The insurgents were moving methodically and swiftly up the mountain toward their hiding place. It wouldn't be too long before they'd be right where the SEALs had been a few days ago when they'd spotted the small cave. The insurgents would have to realize it was an excellent hiding place, and a good place to dig in for an assault.

"Keep eyes on them," Wolf ordered, knowing he really didn't even need to ask Cookie to do so, he'd make sure he knew where every bad guy was to the second.

Wolf scooted backwards awkwardly with one good arm without standing up, not wanting to give their position away prematurely. When he was far enough from the mouth of the cave to move freely, he stood and went over to where Penelope was sitting with Abe.

The thought of his friend being so sick made Wolf's heart hurt, but he put it aside. They had other things to worry about. Abe didn't have a chance if they didn't get out of here alive. And as much as he wanted to be the one helping Abe, he needed Sergeant Turner's help. She wasn't a SEAL, but she *was* a trained soldier.

Wolf looked at Abe and found that at the moment, he was either sleeping or unconscious. He turned to Penelope and saw her eyes boring into his. He laid it out for her. "It's showtime, Tiger. We've got insurgents coming, and coming fast."

"Where do you need me?"

Wolf inwardly smiled. God, this woman was amazing. Every time she opened her mouth, she reminded him of his Ice…and made him all the more determined to get back to her. "What I'm gonna ask you to do will probably piss you off, but I'm not saying it to purposely irritate you." Wolf continued quickly, "I need you to reload for us. I've only got one good arm and can't do it quickly myself."

Wolf watched as Penelope cocked her head and considered his words. His respect for her went up a notch. He saw the moment she reached a decision about her words.

"That makes sense. You guys are better trained for this and probably better shots. I'll do my best to keep up with you. How much ammo do we have?"

Wolf closed his eyes briefly, more thankful than he could ever say that Penelope was the way she was. This entire rescue mission could have gone completely the other direction if she was a different kind of person. Wolf's thoughts went to Cookie and the stories he'd told them about when he'd tromped through the

Mexican jungle with Fiona and the senator's daughter, Julie. Thank God Penelope was more like Fiona than the spoiled, not-prepared-for-any-kind-of-adversity Julie.

Julie had more than made up for her bitchiness though. She'd gone out of her way to apologize not only to Cookie and Fiona, but also to the rest of the team. Wolf never thought he'd be thinking about Julie as a strong woman who simply didn't deal with adversity well, but that's where he was. He brought himself back to the present; he didn't have time to be thinking about the commander's wife and the history between her and the team right now.

He opened his eyes and answered, "Probably not enough, but we'll fight as long as we can. We're trained to make every bullet count. I'm hoping we can knock out the first wave, then make our escape before the next one comes."

"Okay. Help me move Abe back a bit more?" Penelope asked, turning away from Wolf. She had to turn away because she knew if Wolf could see her face, he'd realize how incredibly scared and freaked-out she was. There was no time to give in to it though.

This was it. Do-or-die time.

Wolf came over and helped as best he could with his wounded arm to get Abe settled as far back from the mouth of the cave as possible. They stacked a few of the packs the SEALs had carried from the plane in front of his body to give another layer of protection from any stray bullets that might make their way into their hidey-hole. They worked in silence as Cookie and Benny continued to monitor the movements of the insurgents as they came toward their hiding spot.

"Wolf," Cookie cautioned.

Wolf made his way back to the mouth of the small opening and ungracefully laid himself out next to his teammate, careful to keep his arm as still as possible. Penelope lay on the ground and crawled her way over behind the men. She settled herself between the two of them, so she could reach their empty weapons with ease. It would also be a simple matter of leaning one way or the other to reach the weapons that Benny and Dude had as they stood at the edges of the cave.

"Where's Mozart?" Penelope murmured quickly before things got crazy.

"Recon," Wolf responded curtly, which really told her nothing, but Penelope didn't ask anything else as the first shot rang out in the quiet mountainside.

Penelope startled so badly at that first gunshot, she would've laughed at herself if she had it in her. She ducked down and turned her attention to the men around her. She needed to make sure she was an asset instead of a liability. The last thing she wanted to do was to be a burden on these men. She'd do what she could to help them.

Penelope had no idea how long the firefight lasted. She concentrated on reloading the pistols that were handed back to her when they were empty. She noticed that Cookie had a sniper rifle, thank goodness. It would've been a very different fight without it, a much closer and more personal fight. As it was, the insurgents obviously knew where they were now hiding, but the sniper rifle kept them away from the entrance.

Finally the gunshots tapered off and then stopped altogether.

"Everyone all right?" Wolf asked quietly into the silence.

"Clear."

"Clear."

"Clear."

"I'm good."

The three SEALs and Penelope answered affirmatively.

"Ammo situation?"

The SEALs examined their leftover ammo and the result wasn't good. They each had about three clips for their pistols and Cookie had about twenty more shots with his rifle. Mozart's ammo was still unknown, but Wolf guessed it was probably about the same.

"We've got about an hour, I'm guessing, before the next wave hits. Some of them were bound to have retreated as soon as bullets started flying to get backup and to report our position to the others. We either move up, or try to get past them going down as they're going up."

There was silence for a moment until Benny responded. "I say up. I might be the one with the head injury, but it'll be much easier for a helo to swoop in and snatch us up, the higher we are."

Wolf nodded in immediate agreement. "Let's get the lead out."

"What about Mozart?" Penelope asked, happy to not be a sitting duck in their cave anymore.

"He'll meet up with us," Cookie said with complete confidence.

They packed the bags and had a short discussion about the safest way to get Abe out of the cave and up the mountain. As they were discussing it, he came to. Penelope thought he'd volunteer to be left behind, but she had never hung out with SEALs before. It was obvious he knew his teammates would never, ever leave him behind, so he didn't even suggest it. "I'll help as much as I can. Give me a pistol. If the shit hits the fan, I can at least shoot as you all carry my ass."

Wolf laughed. Penelope couldn't believe anyone could actually laugh about what Abe said, the picture in her mind was anything but funny, but she was finding out that these SEALs were a lot like the guys back home at the firehouse. When they were the most juiced-up on adrenaline and in the midst of danger, they seemed to get more and more crude. It was actually reassuring.

"With our luck, you'd shoot *us* in the ass, Abe."

When the group was ready, Cookie and Dude took Abe by the arms and helped him stand up. He was shaky, and couldn't put any weight on his injured leg, but he was upright. Cookie stuck his shoulder in Abe's armpit and wrapped his arm around Abe's back. Abe wrapped his arm around Cookie's waist and they hobbled toward the entrance to the cave.

Penelope couldn't have stopped the words from coming out of her mouth if her life depended on it. "You two look like you're ready for the world championship three-legged race at the county fair down in Texas." She was relieved that Cookie and Abe both laughed, rather than getting irritated at her inappropriate humor.

"Oh hell yeah, we're *so* entering one of those when we get home, aren't we, Abe?" Cookie said with a smile.

Abe's voice was a bit lower and had less strength, but he responded with, "Yeah, when we get home."

"Okay, Benny will head out first. We'll give him a ten-minute head start. Our radios aren't working for shit, so we'll wait, and if he doesn't come back and tell us otherwise, Tiger, you and Dude will be next, followed by Frick and Frack, and I'll bring up the rear.

Stay low when you get to the top and wait for us to get up there. If something happens, dig in and we'll rendezvous as soon as we can. Got it?"

As everyone agreed, Benny slipped out and disappeared around the side of their hidey-hole. Penelope waited, holding her breath. Ten minutes passed slower than molasses in January. Penelope grimaced at herself. Why she was thinking about corny clichés, she had no idea.

Finally, Wolf gestured at her and Dude. She took a deep breath and headed out behind Dude, sticking as close to him as she'd done when they'd left the tent at the refugee camp.

The first part was the most difficult. Penelope slipped several times, scraping her hands as she caught herself. She had no idea how in the hell Cookie was going to get a semi-conscious Abe up the hill, but she figured if anyone could, it'd be the SEALs. They seemed to be able to do anything, at least from what she'd seen so far.

She made sure to stay behind the small scrub bushes as they passed them, just in case any of the insurgents were still watching. The thought of being shot in the back not a pleasant one.

She'd reached the top of the ridge and looked around, not seeing Benny or Mozart, when she felt an arm wrap around her from behind. A hand covered her mouth and she was pulled into a large, hard body.

She immediately flailed, trying to get away, but she was a beat too slow.

Another arm came around her waist and held her in a grip so tight she had no prayer of moving. The arm around her compressed against her chest, and her cracked ribs. It hurt. Penelope panicked. No, hell no. She hadn't survived all she had to be kidnapped again. She frantically struggled in the tight grip holding her still, to no avail. She felt herself being half dragged and half carried backwards, and there was nothing she could do about it.

Just as Penelope was about to fall into complete despair, she heard Mozart's voice. She looked up and saw six and a half feet of pissed-off Navy SEAL. He had a pistol aimed somewhere above her head. His words were stifled and deadly. "Let her go, asshole, and I might let you live."

Penelope held her breath as the man behind her didn't move.

# Chapter Twenty-Four

*There's still no news of kidnapped U.S. Army Sergeant Penelope Turner. She was kidnapped almost four months ago by ISIS and it's been a while since any video of her has surfaced. We continue to follow this story.*

*In other news, a new reality show premieres tonight featuring men competing to become the ultimate Alaskan. Stay tuned for an interview with one of the contestants.*

CAROLINE TURNED OFF the television in disgust. How anyone could watch that reality show drivel was beyond her. It wasn't as if it was actually real. The only reality show she'd ever been remotely interested in was some sort of dating show set in Australia…at least the man had seemed down-to-earth. She didn't remember how it turned out, but she thought she remembered some sort of scandal, but in the end the man found an actual real love.

Her thoughts were interrupted by the ringing of her cell phone. She headed over to the kitchen counter where she'd left it and picked it up. She recognized the prefix of the Naval base, but not the number itself.

"Hello?"

"Hello, is this Caroline Steel?"

"Yes, who is this?"

"This is Commander Hurt."

"Oh, sorry, Patrick. I didn't recognize your voice." Caroline stiffened suddenly. Oh shit. Why was Wolf's commander calling her? "Is everything all right? Is Julie okay? The guys?"

Ignoring her question, Hurt said solemnly, "I wanted you to hear it from me, rather than the Casualty Assistance Officers who will be showing up at your door within the hour."

Caroline felt her knees give out and she slid to the floor with her back against the kitchen cabinets. She couldn't get any words out.

"Wolf and his team are considered Missing in Action."

Caroline's breath came out in a whoosh. "What?" she whispered.

"MIA. We haven't heard from them since the other SEAL team they were working with reported that they'd completed their mission. They should've been home by now, but we haven't heard anything from them."

Patrick knew he was misleading Caroline a bit, but didn't want to tell her everything he knew…not yet. Tex had given him coordinates of where he thought they were, but until their location had been verified by the Delta Force team, the government was declaring them MIA. The trackers weren't common knowledge and Patrick wasn't going to let that detail slip to Command.

Caroline took in a deep breath. "They're not dead?"

The commander's voice lowered. "We don't know. As of now, they're missing."

Caroline nodded to herself. Okay, this she could deal with. "Then they're just out of pocket. They're not dead. They'll figure it out and get in touch when they can."

"Caroline—"

The commander's tone was sympathetic and a bit pitying, but Caroline didn't let it deter her. "With all due respect, Patrick," she interrupted the senior military official she'd known for a long time, "I appreciate you giving me a head's up. I do. But I'd hope that, as long as you've known Matthew and his team, you'd know that they're tough as hell. Until I see and touch Matthew's cold body for myself, I'll never, ever believe he's dead. Call me naïve, call me idiotic, but I know deep in my heart that they're good at what they do. If there's any way possible they'll be able to make it back home, they will. Even if the odds are a hundred to one. Or a thousand to one. There's still a chance. So if you'll excuse me, I need to start Operation Girl Time and get my posse together. I'm assuming the others will have visitors as well?"

"Yes." The commander's voice held so much respect in that one word, it made Caroline want to weep.

"Okay, then I need to deal with the Navy Officers about to descend on my door, then make some calls to my girls." Her voice softened, sounding uncertain. "You'll keep me informed?"

"Yes ma'am. I'll be sure to call you personally the second I hear anything."

"Thank you. I'll make sure you get an invite to the huge party we're gonna have when our men are home. Deal?"

"Deal. Let me know if you need anything. And I mean *anything*, Caroline. It's the least I can do."

"Just tell me the truth. And keep me informed. That's all I need."

"You got it. Caroline?"

"Yeah?"

"Julie asked if you thought it'd be okay if she came over too. I said I'd talk to you about it. She doesn't want to overstep, but she's worried about all of you."

Caroline swallowed hard. She and the rest of the women hadn't been very nice to Julie when they'd first figured out who she was. Knowing she was the woman who Fiona had spent time with down in Mexico, and who'd been so horrible to her, was a surprising blow to them all. But slowly, Julie had proven that she had changed, and they'd all decided if Fiona could forgive her, so could they.

Besides that, she was now married to Commander Hurt. They saw her all the time and were genuinely thrilled with how happy their husbands' commander was with her. "Yeah, I think we'd like that."

"Thanks. I'll let her know and send her over in a bit."

"Sounds good. I'll talk to you later then? You'll let me know the second you hear something?"

"Of course I will. Bye, Caroline."

Caroline clicked off the phone and laid her head on her knees briefly before stiffening her spine. She had shit to do, there was no time to cry. Hell, there was no reason *to* cry. Every word she'd told the commander came from her gut. Matthew was alive. Everyone was. She had to believe it.

LATER THAT NIGHT, Caroline once again sat in her living room with a full house. She'd been able to catch all of her friends on the phone before they'd had their visits with the officers from the base, except for Fiona.

She'd been out running errands, and had missed both her call and the visit from the base…thankfully.

Alabama had finally gotten ahold of Fiona and told her to drop what she was doing and get her butt over to Caroline's house. She was the last to arrive. Even Julie had made it there before Fiona, and had been just as shocked and upset as the others, but now they sat around talking about what might be happening with their men.

"Caroline, what do you really think is going on?"

Caroline thought hard about Fiona's question, trying to decide what to tell them. She caught Melody's eyes from across the room and her slight nod. She took a deep breath.

"We've never been the type of Navy SEAL wives to question our men, or even to speculate about where they might be when they've been sent on a mission. I don't feel comfortable doing it now, but with what's going on, I feel like I need to."

She looked around at her friends and knew she had their utmost attention. Most of the kids were sleeping. Sara and John were downstairs in the basement, April and Taylor were snoring in their mother's arms, and Akilah was upstairs with Brinique and Davisa, entertaining them as they played with their dolls. It was just the eight of them. Six women who were worried and stressed about the loves of their lives, and Melody and

Julie, who were just as worried that their friends' men wouldn't come home again.

"I'm pretty sure they went over to the Middle East to try to rescue that kidnapped American soldier." Caroline ignored their gasps and continued on quickly, "Matthew didn't tell me, but I kinda guessed, and asked enough leading questions that he actually answered to figure out I was right."

"The helicopter crash?" Summer surmised quietly.

Caroline nodded. "Yeah, I think so."

"But the news reports say there were only four men aboard, and that they were brought to Germany," Cheyenne said.

"Yeah, it doesn't make sense. The only thing I can think of is that chopper was on the way to get them out when it crashed. And Patrick said they were missing, not dead. So I think maybe they've found the woman, and they're just not able to communicate with anyone for some reason. Maybe they're just hunkered down waiting for the right time to come out." Caroline tried to reason what was going on out loud.

"How can they be missing if they have their trackers on? Couldn't Tex just tell the commander where they are?" Jessyka asked the group.

Everyone looked at Melody and Julie. They both looked uncertain.

"Let's leave Melody and Julie out of this," Caroline

told everyone as she pulled out her phone. "It's not fair to put them in the middle. I should've thought of it before, but I'll call Tex and we'll see what, if anything, he can tell us."

Julie piped up before Caroline could get ahold of Tex. "I don't know."

"What?" Summer asked.

"I don't know anything about your husbands. Patrick and I don't talk about his work. I know what he does is extremely sensitive and he could get in big trouble if he told me anything, so I never ask him about it and he never tells me. I would tell you if I knew even the smallest detail. I swear."

"Thanks for that," Alabama said softly. "We appreciate it."

Caroline nodded at Julie and dialed her cell and put it on the coffee table. All eight women hunkered down around it and waited for Tex to answer.

Finally on the fifth ring, he did. "What's up, Caroline?"

"Where are the guys?"

Tex was silent for a moment before he asked, "Why do you ask?"

"Cut the shit, Tex," Fiona said more harshly than she'd ever spoken to Tex before. "I'm sure you already know we were all visited by the base Casualty Assistance Officers today. They've declared Hunter and the others

MIA. But we want to know how they can be missing if they have their trackers on?"

Tex cleared his throat. "You know I can't talk about this, Fee. Even though I'm not active duty anymore, I've still got my government clearance since I work for them, but it's not cool that you're putting me in this position."

"And you know I wouldn't do it if I wasn't completely freaked-out that I'm gonna lose the best man I've ever known, the love of my life, and the lives of the bravest fucking men I've ever met. We're at our wits end here, Tex. God, please. Can't you tell us anything?" Fiona's voice started out hard and unrelenting, but at the end of her impassioned plea, she was near tears.

"Fuck," Tex said. He sighed deeply, obviously effected by Fiona's tone of voice, then said, "Only five of them brought their trackers with them. I can only assume someone forgot it. I doubt whoever it was would deliberately not bring it with him."

"Do you know who forgot it?" Jess asked.

"Yes, but I'm not going to tell you, it doesn't matter," Tex told her.

"So they really are missing then?" Cheyenne's voice was low and strained.

"Sort of."

"Sort of?" Caroline snapped. "Jesus, Tex. You're killing us here. Just spit it out…and in regular English, not any of that coded crap you're so good at."

Tex ignored the snark in Caroline's words, knowing she was stressed-out beyond what most women would be able to handle. She, and all of the women, were actually accepting this very well, all things considered. "They're missing, but I believe I know their general whereabouts. I'm hoping there will be information soon."

There was a lot Tex wanted to tell the women. That there was still a tracker working and he was pretty sure it was with the group. That he'd been in communication with the Delta Force commander and knew they rescued the helicopter crew and were on the trail of Wolf and his men. He hoped the women would trust him to do what was best for their men.

Silence filled the room for a moment before Summer spoke up. "Thank you, Tex. Seriously. I know you told us way more than you should've, but it means everything to us."

"Yeah...Mel?"

Melody spoke up for the first time. "I'm here."

"You still coming home tomorrow?"

Everyone in the room could practically feel the longing in Tex's voice. Sometimes they forgot he was more than just the person who looked over them and kept them safe. He was a father, a husband, and a man who very obviously was feeling the pain of his friends being missing and wanted his wife by his side.

"Yeah. We leave around noon and land around eight your time."

"I'll be at the airport waiting."

"Okay, Tex."

"You ladies need anything else?" Tex asked, obviously asking the other women in the room.

"No, we're as good as we can be at the moment," Alabama told him honestly.

"Okay. For what it's worth, I have a feeling we'll be hearing good news soon," Tex said in a cautiously optimistic tone.

"From your lips to God's ears," Caroline said fervently.

"I'll talk to you guys later." His voice dropped. "See you tomorrow, Mel."

Everyone said their goodbyes and Caroline clicked off the phone. The women stared at each other for a moment before Caroline announced, "Sleepover time. Nobody's going anywhere until our men are found. You too, Julie. You're here, so you're staying. We need all the support we can get."

No one disagreed. They found comfort in being with each other. No one cared that they'd be cramped and things would be crazy with all the bodies in the house. It was better than going home to their empty, lonely homes that would remind them of their missing husbands.

Julie didn't complain, thankful that she'd finally broken through the "acquaintance barrier" that had seemed to stand between her and the other women. Over the couple of years she'd been with Patrick, she'd heard story after story about all of these women and how amazing they were. The fact that Caroline had asked her to stay meant the world. She'd stay with them and support them until their men came home…or through the horror if they never came home at all.

# Chapter Twenty-Five

PENELOPE HELD HER breath and didn't move a muscle. If she could've moved, she still would've stayed right where she was. It wasn't fun looking down the barrel of a gun, even if she knew it wasn't aimed at her. Her attention stayed on the man standing behind her, holding her immobile in his grasp.

"I said, let her the fuck go. Right now." Mozart's voice communicated he was about five seconds away from losing his shit, or blowing someone's head off.

"How about you drop *your* gun, and stop pointing it at my teammate instead?"

Penelope held her breath. Oh jeez. This was quickly turning into a major clusterfuck. There was another man dressed in desert camouflage now holding a gun at *Mozart's* head. She didn't think he was an insurgent, not only because she'd only seen them in whatever raggedy clothes they happened to have, not a uniform, but also because the man had spoken perfect English with only a slight southern twang. But the bottom line was that she had no idea who he was. It would've been humorous if she'd been watching it on television back home, safe in her apartment in San Antonio. But being in the middle of it herself was absolutely *not* funny at all. She couldn't hold back her snarky words, but unfortunately, or fortunately, they came out all garbled because the man behind her still had his hand over her mouth.

Her meaning must've come through, if not her words, because the second man who'd appeared out of nowhere said, "Captain Keane Bryson, Delta Force."

Mozart lowered his pistol immediately and turned to the man. "About fucking time."

They grinned at each other in a weird manly way, as if they hadn't just been about to kill each other two seconds earlier.

Penelope squirmed in the hold of the man behind her again and he finally dropped his arms. She turned to glare at him, shoving against his chest with both arms, annoyed because he didn't even have to step back a foot at her push, before turning back to Mozart and the man who called himself Keane Bryson and saying in a snarky voice, "I don't know how you found us, or what the hell your plan is, but can we *please* get on with it and get the fuck out of here? If you didn't notice, we're not exactly at the Officer's Club on base."

The new guy ignored her and turned to Mozart. "She's got a mouth on her, didn't expect that."

Mozart shrugged and agreed, "She does, but she's one hell of a soldier."

Penelope was ready to throw up her hands in exasperation at the conversation, but at Mozart's words, she could only stare at him dumbfounded. He, a Navy SEAL, thought *she* was a hell of a soldier? Well, okay then.

Mozart held out his hand to the man. "Mozart. Glad you're here. We could use the help. We've got a man down, and the rest of us aren't at a hundred percent."

"Sit rep," the captain requested, now all business.

Before Mozart could respond, Wolf appeared out of the brush. He had his finger on the trigger of his pistol and looked ready to use it before seeing Mozart's signal for friend. Following up behind Wolf was the rest of his team. Penelope was glad to see Abe was still conscious...barely. She went over to Cookie and took some of Abe's weight on herself. She was so much shorter than them she couldn't do much, but she figured every little bit would help.

They all watched as five more men materialized out of the desert landscape. Penelope thought it almost looked like a showdown at the O.K. Corral. Six men lined up on one side, seven on the other.

Wolf gestured toward each of the men on his team. "I'm Wolf, this is Mozart, Benny, and Dude. Abe is the one who looks like he's about to pass out and Cookie is holding him up. You've apparently met Tiger, otherwise known as Sergeant Penelope Turner, formerly a guest of ISIS."

The Army Delta Force men each nodded at the SEALs and their captain introduced them. "I'm Ghost, and this is Fletch, Coach, Hollywood, Beatle, Blade, and Truck."

The testosterone was thick enough on the ridge to choke a horse, but Penelope didn't care. All she cared about was that the odds of them getting out of Turkey, or Iraq, or wherever the hell they were, were just raised about a thousand percent. She would've kissed the Special Forces men if she thought it would've been appropriate at that moment.

Wolf, apparently done with the pleasantries, got down to business. "First, we left four men down near the crash site of the MH-60. Any chance you took care of that?"

"Taken care of," Ghost said matter-of-factly. He didn't elaborate, and Penelope really would've liked to have known more about how they were doing and what was going on with them, but obviously now wasn't the time.

Wolf nodded at Ghost. "Obliged." He continued with the sit rep, "We repelled the first round of insurgents, but expect another any moment. We holed up down there," he gestured back the way they came, "but they obviously found us. We're down to a few clips per person. Abe has a leg wound that needs more medical attention than we've got. My arm is busted. Mozart has an arm wound, but it doesn't seem to be too bad. Benny had a concussion and some bleeding and Dude's ankle isn't a hundred percent."

"And Tiger?" Ghost's words were no-nonsense and clipped.

"Dehydration, hungry, bent ribs, and tough as fucking hell."

Ghost nodded in approval. "Good to know the odds are in our favor."

Penelope gawked at the huge man. Was he high? Wolf had just run through enough issues to make any general cringe, and the dangerous looking man standing in front of her acted as if Wolf had told him they had heat-seeking missiles hidden in their packs. She'd never understand these Special Forces guys. Give her a fireman any day of the week. The ones she worked with might be a bit redneck and a lot country, but at least they weren't fucking crazy.

"Okay, we'll pair up, one of my men with one of yours. They'll hook your guys up with additional ammo. Truck and Blade will take Abe. Sergeant Turner, you stick with me and Wolf. You'll be home before you know it."

Penelope nodded and stepped away from Abe as the two Delta Force men, Blade and Truck, came forward to take him under their shoulders. Cookie nodded at them with respect and gratitude, and the other men got down to business shifting their loads and distributing ammunition.

Penelope was hunkered down between Wolf and Ghost when the first gunshot rang out through the air.

She flinched and ducked, remembering the firefight that they'd lived through not too long ago.

"Easy, sergeant. We've got this," Ghost reassured her with a hand on her shoulder.

Penelope nodded and waited. Surprisingly, Wolf and Ghost didn't even pull out their weapons, but spoke to each other about the plans for extraction as their men shot at insurgents around them.

"You call it in?" Wolf asked Ghost.

"Yeah, an MH-47 is en route."

"Probably best to wait until we take care of this first."

"Yeah, it'll be over before the Chinook gets here."

"From here?"

"Incirlik then Ramstein."

Wolf nodded in approval. "Good. Any chance you can relay a message back home? Our radios are out. Dead batteries."

"Of course."

Wolf leaned toward Ghost and Penelope heard him speaking in what had to be code, because she didn't understand a word of what was said. She was beginning to get irritated and her head reeled, not only from the extremely loud firefight around them, but from confusion as to what was going on and probably a bit of lack of water and food as well.

"Can one of you please translate what the hell is going on?" she demanded, still feeling snarky. Her world was changing too fast for her to keep up and it was extremely confusing and scary.

Ghost laughed, not meanly. "As soon as our boys take care of the assholes, a big-ass helicopter will come and pick us all up. We'll fly to Incirlik U.S. Air Base east of here on the Mediterranean Sea. From there, you'll probably be packed up and shipped off to Ramstein Air Base in Germany. There, you and Wolf's men will get medical attention, then you'll all be headed home."

"Home?" The word soaked into Penelope's psyche like a parasite burrowing in for the long haul.

"Home," Ghost confirmed.

Penelope turned to Wolf with a smile. "Can you tell your guys to hurry the hell up then, we have a chopper to catch."

Wolf smiled down at the petite woman between them. She didn't come to their chin, was dirty and actually pretty disgusting-smelling and looking, but her strong personality and quirkiness came through loud and clear. She might be down, but she sure as hell wasn't out.

"Yes, ma'am," Wolf told her, laughing.

"That's sergeant, not ma'am. I'm not an officer," Penelope told Wolf haughtily, but smiled so he knew she was teasing him.

Wolf didn't answer, but Penelope knew he heard her.

And Ghost was right, it wasn't too much longer before the last gunshot rang out over the mountains. It was almost too quiet. "Is it over?" Penelope whispered into the sudden silence.

"Almost."

# Chapter Twenty-Six

*Stay tuned for a breaking news story out of Germany on the evening news.*

CAROLINE LAY ON her couch with her cell phone in her hand and stared up at the ceiling. Alabama was upstairs in her bed with Brinique and Davisa. Fiona was sleeping in one of the armchairs next to her, and Summer was in the other chair. They'd made a cradle out of a dresser drawer for April, and she was sleeping soundly next to her mother.

Cheyenne and Julie were downstairs in the basement apartment with Taylor, and Jess was in the guestroom with both Sara and John. They were certainly crowded, but not one of the women wanted to be anywhere else.

The kids were resilient and thought it was fun to have a sleepover. Caroline and Fiona had taken Melody and Akilah to the airport the day before. It was always sad to say goodbye to her. Even though she lived on the other side of the country, Melody was still very much a part of their group.

Caroline fingered the cell phone impatiently. She hadn't slept well at all, she had a feeling something was happening. She had no factual basis for the feeling, but it was there nonetheless.

Having the Navy say that Matthew and the other men were "missing," was tough. It was one thing to say goodbye to Matthew every time he left for a mission and not know where he was going or when he'd be back, but she and the other women knew that *someone* knew where they were and what they were doing. But this time, not even the U.S. Navy knew their whereabouts, and that was what freaked her out the most.

Was he hurt? Was anyone else hurt? Caroline refused to believe Matthew was dead. Absolutely refused. As she'd told Commander Hurt, she'd have to see and touch his dead body to believe it…something many SEAL wives never got to do.

Even though Caroline was hoping and praying her phone would ring, she was startled when it actually did vibrate in her grasp. The number came up as "unavailable," but Caroline didn't hesitate to swing her legs over the side of the couch and head into the kitchen and the side door of the house. She didn't want to wake anyone up, but she had a good feeling in her gut about the call.

Caroline eased the door shut behind her and clicked

the phone to answer it before the person on the other end hung up.

"Hello?"

"Ice, it's me."

"Oh thank God! Are you all right? Is everyone else okay?" She could hear the smile in Matthew's voice as he answered her.

"That's my Ice, always worrying about others. We're good."

"Does the commander know where you are? He said you were MIA."

Wolf laughed outright. Caroline had been a Navy spouse for a couple of years now, but she still sometimes was very naïve about how things worked. "Of course he knows, Baby."

"Okay. Can I ask when you guys will be home?"

"I don't know for sure, but I promise it'll be soon."

"Good. Matthew?"

"Yeah, Ice?"

"Can I tell the others?"

"Of course. I told the guys I'd call you. Make sure the others know they'll call as soon as they can, but we've got meetings and stuff we gotta do at the moment."

"I know, I'll tell them. You really are okay?"

Wolf heard the break in his wife's voice and actually felt tears well up in his own eyes. He was a bad-ass

SEAL, but nothing could bring him to his knees faster than his Caroline. "We're all going to be fine."

There was a huge difference in Caroline's mind, but she didn't push it. Right now, *going* to be fine was just as good as fine. "Okay, we'll see you at the base?"

"Probably not. We have to debrief with Hurt and others before we'll be allowed to come home. It'll probably be a couple of days, but I'll text when I'm on my way."

"Okay. Matthew?"

Wolf grinned again. "Yes, Ice?"

"Did you win?"

He knew exactly what she meant and he was proud as fuck that he was able to say, "Yeah, baby. We won."

"Thank God. I love you."

"I love you too."

"I knew you'd find your way home."

"Always. I've got you to come home to. How could I not?"

"Okay, I'm sure you have shit to do." Caroline's voice was back to its usual take-charge tone. "I've got six adults, two toddlers, two babies and two little girls who are going to be getting up any moment now, and will be hungry. Travel safe and I'll see you soon, honey." She could've gone into detail about baby Taylor and Cheyenne's hospital scare and about Jess being pregnant again, but decided her husband had enough on his plate at the moment. Faulkner and the others would learn soon enough all that happened while they were gone. They'd call their wives as soon as they could. It was enough for now that they weren't lost anymore and would be home soon.

"Yes, you will. Stay safe until I get home."

"I will. Love you, bye."

"Bye, Ice."

Caroline clicked off the phone and dropped her head and sighed in relief. Thank God.

# Chapter Twenty-Seven

PENELOPE GRIMACED AT the image staring back at her in the mirror on the base. She and the six SEALs had arrived at the Air Base in Germany without incident. The trip out of the mountains of Turkey had been somewhat anticlimactic. The huge Chinook helicopter swooped down they'd all jumped in, and they'd taken off. And that was that.

They'd landed at Incirlik Air Base in Turkey and Penelope watched as Ghost and his men walked away from the helicopter without a look back. She'd called out, "Ghost!"

The large man had stopped and turned to her.

Penelope had been at a loss for words. What did you say to the man who helped save your life? "Thank you." The words were inadequate, but she hadn't had time to come up with anything else.

Ghost hadn't said a word, but dipped his head in acknowledgement.

Penelope looked behind him and saw that all six of

the other Delta Force men had stopped as well. Maybe they'd been waiting for their leader, but whatever the reason, every single man, one by one, had raised their hand and saluted her. She'd barely seen them through the water filling her eyes.

"I'm not an officer, you can't salute me," she'd managed to get out.

Penelope thought it was the man called Coach who'd replied, "We salute those we respect. And woman, *you* we respect."

*Holy. Shit.* She'd watched as the group of men turned and continued on their way. That was the last she'd seen of the Special Forces team. They'd disappeared into a building on the base and hadn't resurfaced. Penelope had no idea where they'd gone, or what was next on their agenda, but she'd always remember them.

She ran her hand over her short hair. She'd decided that it all needed to come off after her first shower. It was so snarled and disgusting, it was easier to simply cut it short and start over. Penelope had never been the kind of woman to overly worry about her looks. After it was done, she even thought it might be easier to keep it short as a firefighter. Less upkeep and she'd have to worry about it less under her helmet as she worked.

She'd had a long conversation with her brother Cade the first night she'd been in Germany. They'd both cried and Cade had told her all he'd been doing to make sure the government didn't forget about her. She'd also had to meet with the Army lawyers and psychologists. That part wasn't as fun.

Overall, she was exhausted, and feeling a bit claustrophobic. She couldn't go anywhere without someone being right at her side. She didn't want to talk to anyone at the moment, but she also didn't want to be alone. It was ridiculous. She wanted to feel safe, and the one place she'd know she was safe was with the SEALs who'd managed to find her and smuggle her out of the hellhole she'd been in.

Penelope threw on a T-shirt and a pair of Army sweats. She peered out of the barracks room where she'd been housed and didn't see anyone in the hall. Someone had been with her from the second they'd landed through her doctor visit and her brief session with an Army psychologist. It was late, so it was no wonder no one was around, but she kinda expected someone to still be hovering nearby. She tiptoed down the hall as if she was a teenager sneaking out in the middle of the night to meet her boyfriend.

She eased out of the building and made her way across the quiet base, nodding at the security sentry she saw along her way. She'd been introduced to the private when she'd been shown the barracks, and Penelope was glad he recognized her now and didn't ask her any questions about where she might be going. She headed toward the infirmary. She greeted the nurse on duty on the floor she knew Abe was on. She signed in, and headed down to his room.

Penelope knew she was probably given more leeway because of her situation. She'd found out that the American press had dubbed her the Army Princess...which annoyed her to no end. She much preferred Tiger.

She eased open the door to Abe's room and slipped in.

"It's late."

Penelope knew she probably wouldn't be able to sneak in on Abe, but she was still startled at his words. "Yeah."

"Couldn't sleep?"

"Nope."

"Me either."

"How's the leg?"

"Still attached."

Penelope sighed. It was like pulling teeth. "But it's okay?"

"It will be."

"Good."

They were both silent for a moment, until Abe asked, "What's up, Tiger?"

Penelope didn't even try to prevaricate. "Can I sleep

here?"

"Yes." Abe's answer was immediate and, Penelope could tell, heartfelt.

She didn't say anything else, but grabbed two blankets that were on the end of Abe's bed. She laid one on the ground under the window on the far side of Abe's bed, away from the door, lay down, and pulled the other blanket over her. She rested her head on her elbow and sighed in contentment.

She heard Abe moving above her and a pillow suddenly landed on the floor next to her head.

"Take it. I don't need it."

Penelope said, "Thanks," in a soft voice. Nothing else was said between the two military veterans.

Abe listened as the brave Army sergeant fell into sleep and started snoring softly. He didn't like that she was on the floor, but didn't push the issue. She didn't know it, but her actions went a long way toward giving him back his pride. By choosing him over all of his teammates, and putting him between her and the door, and unconsciously letting him protect her, she made him feel better about being unconscious for part of her dangerous rescue.

PENELOPE WAS GLAD none of the SEALs mentioned or gave her shit about sleeping in Abe's room the night before. She'd woken up to quiet conversation and all five of Abe's teammates in the room. She'd forgotten about her hair, and went to brush it away from her face, realizing at the last second that there was no hair there to push out of the way.

She excused herself and used the small restroom off of Abe's room. She finger-brushed her teeth—she'd never take brushing her teeth for granted again—and splashed water on her face. She drank a huge cup of water, then straightened her clothes and stepped back into the room.

"So, when are we heading home?" Penelope asked brightly, hoping the answer would be "today."

"I think you're out of here tonight."

"Awesome," Penelope breathed, hardly able to believe it. She'd been dreaming of seeing Cade again, and stepping foot on her home soil and it looked like it would finally be happening. Then she thought about what Wolf had said. "Wait, *I'm* out of here tonight? What about you guys?"

"We're headed out this morning," Cookie told her.

"We're not going together?" Penelope asked, confused.

"Tiger, you're headed back to Fort Hood in Texas. We're going back to Coronado out in California."

"Oh." Penelope felt stupid. Of course they were. They were Navy, she was Army. Their families were out in California. It still seemed odd, even though she hadn't know these men for long. They'd been through a lot. They'd saved her. It was weird. "Do your wives know you're coming home?"

"Yeah," Wolf answered for all of them.

Penelope suddenly remembered more about their families. "Dude, did your wife have your baby?"

Dude's jaw tightened and he nodded. "Yeah, a healthy baby girl. She was born a couple of days ago."

"I'm sorry you missed it," Penelope told him honestly. "If I hadn't—"

Dude strode over to the small woman who they'd rescued and put a finger over her mouth to shush her. "I might have missed her birth, but she'll be there when I get back. I wouldn't have been anywhere else for the world. And you know what? The day my daughter was born was the same day we pulled you out of that tent. I'd say it was more than worth it."

Penelope stepped away from Dude's touch, and tried to smile at him. God. These men. She knew they were taken, but they were everything she'd ever wanted in a man. They were a bit chauvinistic, a bit heavy-handed, but they weren't afraid to give credit where it was due and she could tell they loved their families with every fiber of their beings. She wanted that. She wanted it more than she'd ever admit to anyone.

"Well, thank you. Thanks to all of you. Seriously.

And you know what? From now on, during the Army-Navy football game…I'm rooting for Navy in tribute to you guys."

Everyone laughed, as she'd hoped they would. She needed the tone to be lightened, and it had been.

"Is it allowed for us to keep in touch? I mean, I know what you guys do is pretty hush-hush, so I didn't know if we could openly communicate with each other or if it'd be frowned on." Penelope watched as the men gave each other indescribable looks. She continued, "Oh, okay, I understand, I was just—"

"Yeah, we'll keep in touch," Wolf interrupted her.

"But, if you'll get in trouble—"

"We'll keep in touch," Wolf repeated, resolutely.

"Okay. I'd like that," Penelope stated, then hurried on. "I have to go…I have an appointment this morning…or something." She knew she couldn't stay there and shoot the shit with these amazing men any longer. She had to make the break. "I'm glad you're all going to be okay…get home to your families." She nodded at each of them and turned and left the room, knowing if she stayed any longer, or if any of them tried to shake her hand or, God forbid, hug her, she'd lose it.

After she left, Benny was the first to speak. "That's one hell of a woman."

"Agreed," Wolf said then changed the subject. "You guys ready to get the hell out of here?"

"Oh fuck yeah," Abe said with enough gusto for all of them.

"Wheels up in two hours. Our women are waiting for us."

# Chapter Twenty-Eight

*As we told you last night, U.S. Army Sergeant Penelope Turner has been rescued from the Middle East. She'd been kidnapped approximately four months ago by ISIS. The three men she'd been taken with were beheaded and burnt and the videotape of their deaths was distributed by ISIS. Turner had been seen on several taped videos extolling the ideology of ISIS and denouncing the Western World's governments.*

*Late this past weekend, a plane touched down at Fort Hood, Texas, with Sergeant Turner, her hair cut short, and flanked by several high-ranking Army officials. She waved from the plane and was hustled into a waiting SUV before being whisked off, most likely to debriefing. She spent a few nights at Ramstein Air Base in Germany before flying back to the States.*

*There has been no word on her rescue or rescuers, but we are hoping to get more details soon. While the Army Princess, as she has been dubbed by the press, has not accepted any interviews, we* will *be talking to Cade Turner, Penelope's brother, next week when he sits down for an exclusive interview. Stay tuned for more details, and let us be the first to say welcome home, Sergeant Turner!*

CAROLINE SAT ALONE in her house and waited impatiently for Matthew to get home. After speaking with him on the phone the other morning, she'd gone back into her house and was happy to let all the others know their men were on the way home.

As usual, they were all gracious and they all understood that it wasn't feasible for all of the guys to call home immediately and talk to them right at that moment. It sucked, but sometimes their job came first, even over family. They all knew they'd call as soon as they could. It was enough for that moment to know they were all safe and on their way home.

Caroline also spoke with Commander Hurt that morning, and he was happy to let her know Matthew was safe and they were going to be on their way home soon. Caroline didn't mention that Matthew had already called her, but she figured he was probably well aware of it.

Julie had pulled her aside before she'd left and let her know that the commander had told Dude about his new daughter. Caroline didn't think Cheyenne would be upset. She knew the guys would've figured she'd had the baby by now.

Caroline and the other women had been texting each other to try to find out when their guys would land, but no one had heard from any of them yet, telling them they were in California, but they all had a feeling it would be soon. Caroline couldn't keep still and she couldn't wait for Matthew to come through the front door.

She was rinsing the plate she'd used for dinner when she heard a key in the squeaky lock from the other side of the house. She spun and for some reason, couldn't get her feet to move. She heard the front door open, then shut, and then heavy footsteps sounded on the wooden floor. Caroline held her breath and then Matthew finally appeared in the doorway to their kitchen. The relief she felt was similar to when she'd seen Matthew appear in her safe house after their plane had been taken over by terrorists.

Caroline drank him in, Matthew looked tired, one arm was in a sling, but he was standing in front of her, and in one piece. She'd take it. She took a step, then another, then another, and then she was in his arms. He'd obviously dropped his bag by the front door, because his good arm wrapped around her and held her tight enough that her feet left the ground. Neither of them said a word, but no words were necessary.

Matthew walked them both over to the couch and sat, never letting go of Caroline. She buried her face in his neck and inhaled, loving his scent, and realizing just how much she missed it when he was gone. She giggled, realizing Matthew had put his nose in her hair and had been inhaling her scent as much as she'd been his.

Finally Caroline pulled back and framed his face with her hands. "I missed you."

"I missed you too, Ice."

"Everyone's really okay?"

"Everyone's really okay."

"Including Sergeant Turner?"

Wolf smiled at his wife. He loved her caring nature. She'd never even met the woman, yet she was full of compassion and concern for her. "From what I've seen on the news, she's fine."

Caroline waited a beat, looking into Matthew's eyes, and knowing she'd pushed him past his comfort point when it came to what he could and couldn't say about his job, let it go. He couldn't exactly admit he knew first-hand how Penelope was doing. She put her head back on Matthew's chest.

"I wouldn't be surprised if we received a Christmas card from Texas in the future, though," he mused, grinning.

Matthew's words surprised her, and she smiled but

didn't lift her head. She was about done talking. Time to show her man how happy she was that he was home.

Caroline brought one hand up to his chest and slowly started undoing his button-up shirt. She slipped her hand under the shirt and played with the skin she'd uncovered. She felt her nipples tighten as she played, just as she felt Matthew get hard under her. She licked his neck and bit down on his earlobe.

"I love you, Matthew," she murmured into his ear. "I missed you. I need you."

As ever a man of few words, Wolf stood up easily, still holding Caroline against his side. "Far be it from me to refuse my wife something she needs," he said easily, striding to their bedroom, not letting go and leaving Caroline to stumble alongside him as she tried to keep up with his large strides.

He laid her down on their bed and crawled on his knees over her as she settled. He put his good hand next to her shoulders and straddled her thighs. He leaned down and touched his forehead to hers. "No matter where I go, no matter what I do, *this* is why I do it. To come home to this. To you. I love you, Caroline Martin Steel. You are my home, my everything. I'd fight through the deepest jungles, the driest deserts, and the widest oceans to end my journey right here in your arms."

Wolf leaned down and kissed away the tears leaking

out of her eyes.

"Less talk and more action please, kind sir," Caroline teased, running her hands up Matthew's chest, pushing his shirt up as she went.

"Yes, ma'am."

No words were spoken for a long while as the SEAL team leader and his wife reaffirmed their love.

ALABAMA SAT WITH Davisa and Brinique and absently watched as they played with their Barbie dolls. They'd been uncharacteristically energetic throughout the day, and Alabama figured it was because they'd somehow sensed Christopher was coming home.

"You're pretty, Mom," Brinique told her out of the blue.

Alabama smiled, realizing again how bright her daughters were. "Thank you, Sweetie. I appreciate it."

Brinique smiled, and kept her eyes on her mom. "Is Daddy coming home today?"

Alabama nodded. "I think so. I'm not sure when, but yeah, I think he'll be home tonight." She had explained to her daughters how Christopher had been hurt, but thought she'd better bring it up again. "You guys remember how I told you Daddy had been hurt while he was away fighting the bad guys, right?"

Both girls nodded solemnly.

"So you have to be careful when he gets here. You can't run into him because he's going to be on crutches. Go easy on him and be careful of his hurt leg. Okay?"

Davisa got up off the floor and went over to Alabama and crawled into her lap. She looked up with her big brown eyes and asked, "We will, Mommy, promise. We'll be really careful."

Alabama hugged her. "I know you will, hon." She squeezed her daughter, and they both looked up when they heard a noise at their front door.

"Daddy!" Brinique screeched, springing up from the floor with an ease only a six-year-old could know and racing toward the front of the house.

Davisa squirmed off of Alabama's lap and hurried after her sister. Alabama quickly followed and held her breath at the first glimpse of her husband after a very long and stressful mission. He was standing with both arms around his girls, with a pair of crutches balanced precariously under his armpits. He looked a bit pale to Alabama, but otherwise unscathed. He was wearing khaki pants and a button-up shirt. There was a faint tan line on his face where a beard had recently been scraped off, but it was the pain lines around his eyes that made her go to him.

She moved to his side and grabbed one of the crutches, propping it up against the wall. She put her shoulder under him and wrapped her arm around his back. Looking up, she murmured, "Welcome home, Christopher."

Abe looked down at the three females in his life and felt his heart expand. God, he'd almost fucked this up a few years ago. He'd almost let this…perfection…slip through his fingers. He thanked God every single day for getting a second chance, that Alabama had *given* him a second chance. Abe lowered his head and brushed his lips across his wife's, relishing the taste and feel of her under him. "Thanks. It's good to be home."

"Daddy, Daddy, we got Barbies!" Davisa shrieked. "Aunt Caroline found them in a box and said we could play with them for as long as we wanted!" She continued, "And Aunt Jess has been throwing up *every day*, and Aunt Cheyenne named her baby Taylor just like I said, and—"

Brinique interrupted her sister. "It's *my* turn to talk. Daddy, I can write the entire alphabet and I'm in charge of brushing my own teeth now, and Akilah taught me how to say 'I love you' in Iraqi and we miiiiissed you."

Abe smiled down at his girls. He'd missed their nonstop chatter more than he'd realized until right this moment.

"Come on, girls, let's let Daddy come in and sit, shall we?" Alabama asked rhetorically, already moving the reunion party farther into the house. She got Christopher settled on the couch, helping him prop his leg onto an ottoman, and they spent the next hour catching each other up with their lives.

Finally the time came for Brinique and Davisa to go to bed. Abe read them two stories and kissed them each on the forehead. "The sooner you go to sleep, the sooner a new day will come." The familiar words seemed to soothe the girls and Abe could hear them snoring before he shut the door behind him.

Abe knew the hardest conversation was still to come. He knew when he sat, he'd be down for the night, so he hobbled into the bathroom to take care of business and then made his way into the bedroom. Alabama was already changed into one of his T-shirts for bed. She put one hand on his face as she went to the bathroom. "I'll be out in a moment. Get comfortable."

Abe nodded and watched with gratitude as his wife went into the bathroom. He quickly stripped off his clothes until he was nude. He needed the closeness being skin to skin with Alabama would bring tonight.

He lay on the bed and didn't bother pulling the covers up and over his legs. He knew Alabama would need to see for herself his injury and make sure he was all right. He didn't begrudge her that in the least.

Alabama came out of the bathroom and over to their bed. Without a word, she sat on the side next to Christopher's injured leg and brushed her fingertips over the still-healing wound, which was covered in a thick bandage.

Abe didn't say anything, he simply let his wife reassure herself that he was there, and was all right. He'd been injured before, but not like this. He hated to seem weak in front of Alabama, but he knew she needed this.

Finally, after another few minutes, Alabama leaned down and kissed the skin above and below the bandage, then she stood up, removed the shirt she was wearing, and climbed into bed. She didn't bother crossing over to the other side, she carefully crawled over him by straddling his knees and moving to his other side. She pulled the covers out from under him and pulled the sheet over them both.

Abe wrapped an arm under her shoulders and sighed in pure contentment as Alabama lay her head on his shoulder and wrapped her free arm over his belly.

"Welcome home, Christopher," she said softly, running her fingers over and around his belly button.

"Thank you. It's good to be home."

"The girls missed you. *I* missed you."

"I missed you too."

"You're really all right?"

"Yeah. To be honest, I missed most of the exciting stuff 'cos I was either high on the pain killers the guys kept forcing into me or passed out, but I'm good. The team took care of me and I'm here and in one piece." Abe didn't censor his words too much. He always wanted to be honest with Alabama, as much as he could be while not worrying her further or breaking his top-secret clearance with the government.

He inhaled as Alabama's hand lowered. When she circled him and squeezed, he stopped breathing. "Alabama…"

"I figured you needed a proper welcome home. I'm not hurting your leg, am I?"

"Fuck no. This would never hurt me."

Alabama chuckled and shifted in his grasp. She felt Christopher hold his breath as she moved down his body and kneeled next to his hip. She glanced up at him as her hands fondled his now hardening shaft. "Well, let me know if I *do* hurt you…" And she lowered her head, doing what she'd dreamed of the many nights that her husband had been gone. She'd always loved taking him in her mouth. He was the only man she'd gone down on, and she loved that she could make him lose his tightly held control when she did this for him.

Fifteen minutes later, Alabama snuggled up next to Christopher again, listening as his breathing settled into a normal pattern again. She smiled against him.

"Jesus, woman. You're gonna kill me."

"But what a way to go, huh?"

"Yeah. I love you."

"I love you too."

"The only thing on my mind while I was out there,

lying wounded and not knowing how things would turn out, was you. You're everything to me. *Everything.* I love you," Abe told Alabama, his words quiet in the dark room.

"Christopher—"

"No, I know you know, but I want you to *know* that you've burrowed yourself so far into my heart that you'll always be there."

"Seriously, Christopher—"

Abe didn't give her a chance to finish. "Now..." He tightened his hold on her shoulders and urged her to roll onto him. "Come up here and let me show you how much you mean to me."

Alabama felt her insides moisten as she straddled Christopher's stomach. "I don't want to hurt you."

"As much as I hate to admit it, I'm not up for making love yet, but," he put his hands on her ass and pulled her forward, "I *am* up for this. Let me taste you, babe. Let me *show* you how much you're loved."

Alabama didn't say anything else, she simply did as she was told. She held on to their headboard as Christopher did indeed show her how much he loved her and how much he'd missed her.

FIONA SAT OUTSIDE on her front porch, not wanting to miss Hunter when he pulled up. She knew he'd be coming home soon, and as much as she wanted to know the exact time, there was something about the anticipation coursing through her belly that made this moment unlike anything she'd ever experienced before.

She hadn't been able to eat anything earlier because of her excitement, but she could now hear her belly growling. There was no question of whether or not she'd leave her post to grab something. She wasn't leaving until Hunter was in her arms.

The light was leaving the sky when Fiona finally heard the sound she'd been waiting for. She stood up and watched as Hunter's truck came rumbling down the street. She stepped off the porch and waited on the grass next to the steps until he stopped the vehicle. Then she was there as he turned the engine off and reached for the door handle. She took a step backward to allow Hunter to open the door, but didn't give him a chance to get out.

Fiona threw her arms around Hunter's waist and held on as tightly as she could.

Cookie swallowed the lump in his throat. It would never get old to be welcomed as honestly and joyfully as Fiona always welcomed him home. He put his arms around her shoulders, waiting for her to get her initial rush of tears out of the way. She always cried when she first saw him.

Finally she pulled her head back and looked up at

him. Fuck, he was the luckiest man alive. She was beautiful with her eyes wet with tears and the small smile on her face.

"Welcome home, Hunter."

"Thank you, Fee." He waited, then smiled when she didn't say anything else and didn't move. "You gonna let me get out or are we going to stay out here all night?"

She smiled but didn't move. He smiled back. So be it. He put his hands under her arms and hauled her up and onto him until she was straddling him on the seat. It was a tight fit because of the steering wheel next to his arm, but she didn't seem to care. She wrapped her arms around him and buried her face in his neck.

Cookie shifted his weight and turned with one hand on the small of Fiona's back she was resting against the steering wheel. He leaned over and shut the door to the truck, then reached down and pulled the level that shifted the seat until it was as far back as it could go. Finally Fiona pulled back and smiled down at him.

"Are we going somewhere?"

"No, but you didn't seem to be in any hurry to go inside, and I'm content holding you in my arms no matter where we are, so right here is as good a place as any to make love to my wife."

"Hunter!" Fiona groused without heat. "We can't make love out here."

"Why not?"

"Well…because. We're outside. It's still light."

"It won't be light for long." Cookie put both hands on her jaw and looked into her eyes. "I love you, Fee. You're a sight for sore eyes."

Fiona stopped complaining; hell, she was happy right where she was. She moved her hips forward and nudged against his hard shaft. She'd missed him, but she'd also missed his body. She never thought she'd become as comfortable with her sexuality as she was after all she'd been through, but she believed deep down it was because she trusted Hunter explicitly. He took things slowly with her and made sure she was comfortable with anything they did together. He'd even gone to the clinic and stayed with her every second as she'd had blood drawn and been examined for any sexually transmitted diseases. By some miracle, she'd escaped any physical long-term effects of her time south of the border. And mentally, she was as whole as she was because of the man sitting in front of her.

"I love you too, Hunter. Is everything okay? Is that girl all right?"

Cookie gave Fiona a weird look. He hadn't told her anything about the mission, but obviously she knew, had figured out, some of what they'd done and where they'd been. Knowing she never would've brought up the issue if it hadn't been for her own history, Cookie told her what he could, while still retaining the confidentiality of the mission. "Yeah, she's amazing, actually. She reminded me a lot of you. No complaints and she did what she had to do."

Fiona sighed in relief. God, she was happy to have Hunter home. She reached down and worked on releasing him from the confines of his pants. "You're right. It's getting dark, we're on private property, and our neighbors aren't close enough to see us. I need you."

Cookie smiled and leaned back in the seat as far as he could, giving his wife room to work. "I need you too," he groaned when Fee finally pulled him free of his pants. He looked down to watch her stroking him.

She looked up and licked her lips seductively. "Help me get out of my pants?"

Cookie leaned over, without breaking eye contact and rummaged into the side pocket of his duffle bag sitting on the seat next to him until he found his KA-BAR knife. He flicked it open and reached for the waistband of her yoga pants. "These aren't your favorites, are they?" he asked.

"No. But even if they were, I wouldn't care. Do it." Cutting her clothes off wasn't exactly the help she'd been expecting, but she'd take it if it meant getting her husband inside her quicker.

Cookie took his time and ran the knife down the cotton of her pants, easily slicing through them. She wasn't wearing any underwear, which made him even harder in her grip than he was before.

"Lift up," he demanded.

Fiona came up on her knees and Cookie pulled at her ruined clothes until he could see to the heart of her.

"Fucking beautiful," Cookie murmured, closing his knife and blindly throwing it toward his bag on the seat, not taking his eyes off of Fiona. He brought his hand down and found her soaking-wet folds. With the other hand, he shoved up her shirt and palmed her naked breast, feeling her nipple peak at his touch.

"This is gonna be fast, Fee. It's been too long since I've been inside you."

"Oh yeah, do it. I'm ready," she breathed, panting.

Cookie brushed her hand away from him and ordered, "Hold on to me." When she put both hands on his shoulders, he took himself in his hand and palmed his wife's ass. "Lift up and scoot forward."

Fiona did as he asked and after he'd notched himself where he most wanted to be, he let go and took both her ass cheeks in his hands.

Fiona didn't wait for Hunter to make the next move, she dropped down onto him and ground her pelvis forward, seating him as far inside her as he could go.

"Jesus, fuck," Cookie groaned.

"God, yes," Fiona said at the same time. She tangled her fingers into his too-long hair, remotely taking note that he needed a haircut, and slowly lifted her hips before slamming down. She did it again, and then again before Hunter took over their rhythm.

He moved his hands from her ass to the sides of her hips and gripped her hard enough to leave marks. Neither cared. It was a tight fit, and they couldn't move more than a few inches, but it was enough.

When Cookie felt himself getting close to losing it, and realized Fiona wasn't quite there yet, he ordered, "Take yourself there, Fee. Do it."

He watched as she straightened her spine and sat up on his lap. She moved one of her hands down to where they were joined and used their fluids to coat her fingers before touching herself. She moaned and threw her head back as she continued to quickly flick against her bundle of nerves.

Cookie could tell she was getting close by the way her body gripped him rhythmically. "That's it, Fee. That's it. You're so beautiful. I'm the luckiest bastard in the world. Fuck me, Beautiful. Take me."

At his last words, he felt Fiona grind down on him and hunch into his chest. Her muscles sucked him in and squeezed him so hard he groaned. He lost it and couldn't help his hips from thrusting up once, then again as he emptied himself inside the most beautiful woman he'd ever known, inside and out.

Neither moved, enjoying the closeness and intimacy

between them after being apart for so long.

"I love you, Fee," Cookie told his wife, shoving one hand up and under her shirt to rest on her back. The other moved to her ass, holding her to him.

"I love you too. More than I think I'll ever be able to put into words."

SUMMER WOKE UP slowly, wondering what had disturbed her. She didn't hear April fussing on the baby monitor next to their bed, so wasn't sure what was going on for a moment.

"Hi, Sunshine."

The words were hushed and spoken right next to her. Summer looked up into the eyes of her husband. "Sam," she breathed, trying to clear her sleep-muzzled head. "You're home."

"I'm home," he said simply.

Summer scooted up until her back rested against the headboard. She reached out and hauled Sam into her arms, loving how great it felt to have him home again. She realized he was wearing only a pair of sweats, and no shirt when she felt the crisp hairs of his chest against her cheek. She pulled back and looked up. "How long have you been home?"

"About ten minutes. I looked in on April, then came in here, took off my shirt and I've been sitting here watching you sleep for the last five minutes or so."

"I meant to be awake when you got here, but April has been fussy and waking up more often at night."

"Probably because she feels your stress. She'll sleep better now that I'm home," Mozart said with a bit of arrogance.

Summer would've called him on it, but he was most likely right.

"It looks like I got here just in time though," Mozart said, looking down at Summer's chest.

She looked down and blushed, even though it wasn't the first time her breasts had leaked in front of her husband.

"I'll go get April, settle in," he told her, standing up.

Summer saw the bandage on his arm for the first time. "Sam, your arm! Are you okay?"

"It's nothing. Swear. I'll let you examine it tomorrow."

Satisfied he was telling the truth, Summer nodded. "Okay. Now, go get our daughter before I flood the place."

Sam left the room and returned with April cradled in his arms. Summer moved over and picked up the nursing pillow. Sam put April on it and flicked open the buttons to the shirt Summer was wearing. He parted the material and held up her breast as Summer guided April to her chest.

Mozart settled down deeper into the pillows next to his wife and watched his daughter nurse. It wasn't something he ever thought he'd be interested in watching, but he couldn't get enough of it now. It was amazing to see Summer nurturing his daughter in front of his eyes. April's lips suckled and pursed as she nursed. Her little fist clenched against her mom's upper breast as she fed.

Mozart looked up into Summer's eyes. She was watching him, not April. "You like this," she stated.

Mozart could only nod.

She smiled at him. God, she loved this man. "Switch sides?" she asked, and watched as he turned April and readjusted the pillow. He again held her breast up while Summer guided April's mouth to her breast. Sam's head was right next to his daughter's now and he stroked her head as she fed. When she was full, April's mouth fell away from Summer's nipple.

Mozart ran a finger over the tip of Summer's breast and wiped away a stray drop of milk. "Fucking beautiful," he muttered, before reaching for April. He brought his infant up to his shoulder and stood. "I'll burp her and put her back down. I'll be back. Don't move."

When Summer went to pull her shirt back together, Sam stopped her. "I said, don't move. Not an inch." Summer smiled up at her husband and put her hands back at her sides. "Okay, honey. Hurry back."

Sam was back within five minutes. Without a word, he stripped his sweats off and climbed into bed next to her, completely naked. It was obvious he was happy to see her.

He pulled the shirt she'd been wearing the rest of the way off her shoulders and eased Summer down flat on the bed.

Mozart nuzzled his wife's breasts, loving the sweet smell of milk that lingered after April had fed. He wasn't interested in the milk she could produce, but he *was* interested in how sensitive her breasts were. He pinched both nipples gently, watching as a bit of milk came out of each breast. She squirmed under him, and Mozart smiled. Oh yeah, he loved how sensitive she was.

"I love you, Summer. You're the most beautiful person I've ever seen in my life."

"You're just horny."

Mozart didn't get upset, just smiled wider at his wife. "That too, but that's not why I think you're the most beautiful woman I've ever seen. It's because you just are."

"Yeah, I smell a little funky, and I manage to ruin half the clothes I wear because I can't stop lactating. I've got stretch marks all—"

Her words were cut off when Mozart put his hand over her mouth lightly. "You have stretch marks because you were carrying my child. I don't care how many clothes you ruin, I'll buy you more. You have no idea how amazing it is to watch April suckle from your breast. I understand why some people have kinky baby/mommy fantasies now."

Summer laughed and Mozart continued.

"You carried my child for nine months and you now nourish her. That's a miracle. You are *my* miracle. I know we might not ever have another child because we're concerned about your age, but it doesn't matter. I have you and I have April. I can die a lucky man."

Mozart moved his hand from Summer's mouth and hovered over her, loving how she immediately spread her legs to give him room. He settled himself and reached down to ease himself inside her already wet folds. He kept one hand on her right breast, kneading and caressing her, ignoring the liquid that oozed out and down her side onto the sheet below them.

They were both lost in the moment of being together again after a long, terrifying separation. "You're the love of my life. I adore you, Summer."

Summer arched into Sam's arms, not feeling one iota of embarrassment about her body and what Sam was doing to it. Everything they did was natural and loving. "I love you too, Sam Reed. Always and forever."

"Always and forever," Mozart repeated, making love to his wife as if it was the first time all over again.

DUDE STRODE INTO his house, dropping his bag on the floor without a thought. He needed to see Cheyenne. After hearing all she'd been though and realizing how close he'd come to almost losing her, all he wanted to do was hold her in his arms.

"Shy!" he bellowed, trying to find her.

"For God's sake, Faulkner, hush! I just got her down!" Cheyenne scolded as she popped her head out of their bedroom.

Dude felt his breath stutter and his heart literally stop beating for a moment. Seeing Cheyenne upright and healthy looking brought it home to him that she really was all right. He'd half imagined he'd find her in bed, pale and sickly. He should've known. His Shy wouldn't let anything keep her down for long.

He headed for her, and she must've seen something in his eyes, because she backed away from him as he entered their bedroom. She backed up until her knees hit their bed and she sat down hard.

Dude didn't stop, but came at her until he was over her with his hands on the mattress at her hips. He leaned over and took her mouth without a word. Loving that she immediately submitted to his kiss, Dude felt himself grow hard against her.

It was still way too soon to take her the way he really wanted and needed to, though. She'd had his baby not a week earlier, and had been through hell in the process.

Dude breathed through his nose and tried to calm himself down. There'd be time later to tie her to their bed and make her explode over and over before burying himself in her heat.

He pulled back. "We aren't having any more babies." It wasn't what he thought he was going to say, but as soon as he said it, it felt right. There was no way he was going to risk her life again. No fucking way.

"Faulkner, I'm fine." Cheyenne put her hand on her husband's chest and stroked him, trying to ease his worries.

"Don't care. No more babies."

Cheyenne decided to let it go for now. After seeing Taylor, she knew she wanted more. She'd just have to give Faulkner time to get to know and love Taylor. He'd want a son, she knew it. They'd just have to keep trying until that happened.

"Do you want to meet your daughter?" Cheyenne asked Faulkner gently.

He blinked. It was obvious he'd been so intent on seeing her and making sure she was all right, he hadn't even remembered he *had* a daughter.

"Christ. Yeah," he whispered.

"Help me up," Cheyenne told him.

He did and she kept hold of his hand and led him over to the crib in the corner of their room. Taylor was sleeping soundly. Cheyenne watched as Faulkner leaned over the crib to look more closely at the baby.

"Can I pick her up?" he asked in an awed whisper.

Cheyenne held back the laugh that threatened. "Of course," she told him. "Just be sure to support her head."

Dude reached for his daughter and put one hand under her head and the other under her back. His hands were so big just one covered her entire back and most of her butt as well. He lifted her up and cradled her to his chest. He looked around and brought her over to their bed.

He gently put her down and started unsnapping her onesie. He knew Cheyenne was watching him carefully, but he didn't let it deter him. He pulled one arm, then the other out of her clothes and eased the material down her little body and off. He un-taped her tiny diaper and moved it to the side.

Dude couldn't believe how small and perfect the little human was, lying on the bed where she was conceived. He leaned down and nuzzled her little foot. Then he ran his pinkie, which still looked huge, up her leg to her waist. He marveled at her still-healing belly button.

"An outie," he breathed, looking at Cheyenne for the first time.

She smiled and simply nodded.

Dude turned his attention back to his daughter. He

put his finger in her palm and felt his heart clench when she immediately clutched it tightly. He looked over her face. Her button nose, the little patch of dark hair on her head, her tiny perfect ears. Her lips pursed and she squirmed a bit as he watched.

Cheyenne appeared next to him and handed him a soft, fuzzy blanket. "Better wrap her up so she doesn't get cold. You don't want to wake her up."

Dude held the blanket and looked down at his daughter. He wasn't sure how to swaddle her. "Help me?" he asked Cheyenne.

He watched as his wife made quick work of wrapping up their daughter until she resembled a small burrito. She held her out to him. Dude took her and looked down at the little miracle resting in the crook of his arms.

Cheyenne sat next to him on the bed and said, "Faulkner Cooper, meet your daughter, Taylor Caroline Cooper."

Cheyenne never thought she'd ever see her big, bad, dominant, overbearing, controlling SEAL of a husband cry, but sitting next to him, watching as the tears fell from his eyes and landed on the blanket holding their daughter, was a moment she knew she'd never forget, and would hold dear for the rest of her life.

JESS LEANED AGAINST Kason's car at the Naval base. She'd had the balls to call Commander Hurt and demand to know when her husband would be home. He must've felt some remorse about the entire situation and how they'd all been declared MIA, because he told her they should be heading home by early evening.

Jessyka had taken a taxi to the base to wait for him. She didn't have the patience to wait at home. She wanted to see him as soon as possible, and if that meant she took her ass to him, then so be it. It wasn't the most practical thing she'd ever done in her life, but she didn't care.

She'd taken Sara and John out to eat first. They'd stuffed themselves with chicken fingers then played on the playground at the fast-food place. Then she'd taken them to the park on the Naval base and let them run around even longer.

She'd even forgone their usual nap, not caring they had reached their limit and were grumpy as hell. After the taxi had driven around the parking lot until they'd found Benny's car, Jess had strapped their sleepy bodies into their car seats she'd brought with her, turned on a kids' movie on their tablets, and they were now sleeping the sleep of full and extremely tired toddlers.

Benny walked quickly toward his car, wanting nothing more than to get home to Jess and the kids. He wasn't paying attention, something that could get him killed if he'd been on a mission, but in the middle of a public parking lot at the base, he wasn't too concerned. He'd reached into his pocket to fish out his keys when he heard a feminine voice say, "Hey."

He looked up and gawked. What the hell was Jess doing here?

He didn't care. He surged forward and snatched his wife up in his arms, twirling her around and around, loving her laugh ringing through the parking lot. He lowered her until her feet hit the ground.

"Where're the kids?"

She gestured to the car behind them with her head. Benny turned and looked, seeing his son and daughter sleeping soundly in the back seat, the slight breeze ruffling their hair from the open windows. He turned back to Jess and lowered his head.

She met him halfway and they made out in the parking lot as if they were back in high school. Finally, when Benny felt Jess's hand move over the front of his jeans, he knew he had to pull back. It seemed that Jess was the horn dog in their relationship, and he loved it.

"It's great to see you, Jess. It's *so* good to see you."

"Are you all right?" Jessyka asked, fingering the bandage on the back of his head.

"Yeah, you know how hard my head is." Jess smiled at him. "You should've waited at home. I'm sure it was a pain in the butt to lug those two all the way out here."

"I couldn't wait. I wanted to see you as soon as possible. The extra twenty minutes it would've taken you to get home would've been twenty more minutes I'd've had to wait to see you." She cleared her throat before continuing. "And I have something I wanted to tell you."

Benny stiffened. It was never good when a woman said she wanted to talk. To be fair, Jess hadn't exactly said those words, but that's what he heard. "What is it? Is everyone okay? The girls? Oh shit, the other kids?"

Jess soothed Kason by running her hands down his shirt. "Everyone's fine. It's nothing like that." She watched as he let out the breath he'd obviously been holding.

"Then what is it? What was so important that it couldn't wait until I got home?"

"I'm pregnant." Jess didn't mince words.

"What?"

"Pregnant. It looks like you have the most determined sperm in the history of mankind. Of course, I'm not really surprised, considering they belong to you, but still. We were going to wait, but I guess that plan is shot to hell."

"You're pregnant?"

"Yeah, that's what I've been telling you." Now Jess started to get nervous. Kason hadn't said much. Maybe he was upset?

"Fuck, woman. I love you so much it's not even funny!"

Jess smiled even as Kason was kissing her again. He obviously wasn't upset.

Benny pulled back from his wife, and looked her in the eyes. "I love you. I love that I've knocked you up again. I know it's hard on you to have so many young kids in the house, and I'd already decided to hire a nanny to help you out, but you should know, I plan on keeping you pregnant as much as I can. I want as many kids as you'll let me get away with. I want a huge family, full of laughter, smiles, drama, tears, toys, shit on the floor, arguments over who gets to use the bathroom, and general mayhem. I know I can't bring Tabitha back, and I can't ever take away that hurt, but I love that your womb was made for my sperm."

Jess rolled her eyes. Kason could be such a dork, but at the same time sweet too. "As long as it's safe, and we have healthy kids, I'm not adverse to a big family. But Kason, don't think I'll be like that huge family on television where the mom is having kids into her sixties or whatever."

"Deal." Benny smiled huge and leaned in to Jess to whisper in her ear. "And I love how horny you get when you're pregnant. Bonus for me."

"Kason!" Jess scolded even as he brought her to him again.

"I'm going to take you home, put our kids to bed, then fuck you until you can't walk."

Jess simply shook her head. She loved this man. He was her everything.

JULIE SNUGGLED UP next to Patrick on the couch. "Is Penelope all right?"

Patrick tightened his arm around his wife. He knew she'd need to know about the kidnapped sergeant, and she'd been very patient and hadn't asked. He carefully worded his answer so as not to break his security clearance.

Hell, who was he kidding? He'd already broken it, he just hoped not to smash it into smithereens.

"She's good, Julie."

"Did she…" Julie stopped and cleared her throat and tried again. "Did she handle the rescue all right?"

Patrick's heart about broke at the question. He knew Julie still had feelings of guilt over how she'd acted when *she'd* been rescued by the team. She's mostly worked through them, but it wasn't surprising that this mission brought her insecurities back to the surface. He nodded, then pushed Julie until she was lying on her back on the couch and he moved up so he was hovering over her.

"She was scared, but she was fine. The guys took care of her. But, Julie, it's going to affect her. No one can go through what she…and you…went through and not be affected. You've talked about this with Dr. Hancock, everyone deals with things differently."

Julie bit her lip and looked away from him. Patrick put his hand on her cheek and pulled her lip away from her teeth. "Look at me, honey."

When she lifted her eyes to him, he continued. "I love you. You can be all take-no-prisoners one minute, and the next you're sitting in a room full of teenagers trying on prom dresses, giggling and laughing. Let it go. You're here. You're mine, and I'm not letting you go."

She nodded up at him. "Okay, Patrick. Thank you. I try not to compare myself…but sometimes it's hard."

"I know, but you were with the girls this week and it was all good."

"Yeah, it was. I finally feel like they've truly forgiven me. I was happy to be there for them and that I could help out when they were so worried."

"Good. Now…there's something else I wanted to talk to you about…"

"Yeah? Is everything all right?" Julie looked into Patrick's eyes worriedly.

"Everything is fine…except we haven't been able to spend much one-on-one time together recently. But after this mission, the guys have been given a mandatory two-week convalescence leave. And although I command two other SEAL teams, I've also been granted those two weeks as well…" His voice trailed off as the smile crept across Julie's face.

"Really?" she breathed. "Two whole weeks?"

"Yup. Think you can take the time off from the store?"

"Hell yeah. I own the thing, I'm sure I can manage to sneak away. Oh, Patrick, I'm so excited to spend time with you!"

"We'd better get some sleep," Patrick told her with a smirk.

"What? Why?"

"Because tomorrow we're going to be busy packing and doing last-minutes errands. I'm sure you'll have instructions for your staff."

"Packing? For what?"

"We're headed to Hawaii the day after tomorrow."

Patrick smiled and sat up as Julie screeched and wiggled out from under him on the couch. "Oh my God! Are you serious? I've always wanted to go to Hawaii!"

"I know."

It was as if he hadn't spoken. "I have a million things to do! I need to—"

Julie's words were cut off before she could get going. Patrick swung her over his shoulder and strode for their bedroom door. He knew if he let her get all worked up now, she wouldn't get to sleep for hours…and he had plans.

"Patrick, let me down! I have to—"

"What you have to do is let me love you. Let me show you how much you mean to me. We'll get a good night's sleep…after…and then tomorrow you can worry about packing." He dumped her gently on their bed and caged her down with his body and arms.

"I love you, Julie Hurt. I know you worry about the team, and their women, but I want to give you ten days of worry-free vacation time. Just you and me."

Julie put both her hands on Patrick's face. "I love you. Thank you for seeing the good in me, even when I wasn't sure it was really there. I'd be more than willing to stay here in our house, in our bed, with you for ten days, but Hawaii? You're so getting lucky, mister."

Patrick smiled down at his wife. "I'm counting on it, Babe." He leaned down and kissed his wife, and neither came up for air for a good long while.

MELODY THREW HER head back and tried to get some much-needed air into her lungs. She gripped Tex's sides, knowing she was probably leaving marks on his skin, but not caring. Every time he thrust his hips forward, he rubbed against the bundle of nerves at the top of her mound to make her cry out.

When he scooted forward and pulled her ass farther up onto his lap, Melody's eyes popped open and she looked up. Tex had an intense look on his face as he looked down to where they were joined. He moved one hand and put his thumb over her clit and rubbed her hard as he continued to shift his hips back and forth.

"If you aren't already pregnant, you will be after tonight, I can feel it. Take my seed, Mel. Take it."

Melody couldn't have stopped the words from flowing out of her mouth if her life had depended on it. She and Tex had always had a healthy sex life, but now that there was the possibility she could get pregnant, Tex seemed to be even more vigorous. "Yeah, I want it. Give it to me, Tex. Give me your baby."

"Oh fuck, Mel. I love you so much." Tex's words were torn from his throat as he planted himself inside her as far as he could go and frantically rubbed her most sensitive spot. "Come with me, Mel. Squeeze me dry."

That was it; that was all it took. Mel's back bowed and felt herself squeeze Tex as she exploded in orgasm. She shuddered and shook, and it wasn't until much later that she realized Tex hadn't pulled out or otherwise moved.

She could feel that he wasn't hard anymore, but he hadn't made any move to change position. Melody stretched and arched her back, throwing her arms over her head, enjoying the look of lust in her husband's eyes as he took in her body below him. "Usually we're snuggling by now," Melody said lightly, keeping her arms above her head.

"I want to keep my sperm inside you as long as possible," Tex said in a low voice.

Melody laughed, and felt Tex slip out of her.

"Oh man, you weren't supposed to laugh, Mel."

She couldn't help it—that made her giggle more. Her laughter stopped when she felt Tex's finger entering her and swirling in their combined juices. "You don't think you're pushing it all back in, do you?" she managed to ask semi-seriously, eyeing Tex as he didn't take his gaze from her sex.

"No. Okay…maybe."

Melody smiled again. Sometimes he acted so far from the bad-ass SEAL he used to be, she couldn't even imagine him on a mission. She had no doubt he was as lethal as any SEAL could be, she'd seen him in action when Diane had threatened her life, but it was times like this she treasured the most. "Come here, Tex. Snuggle with me."

Tex scooted backward and let Mel's legs drop. He immediately turned her onto her side and spooned her from behind. One hand went under her head, and the other went to cup her sex gently. They lay like that for quite a while and Melody even dozed a bit before Tex finally spoke.

"All my life I've been told how smart and talented I am. I joined the Navy and was told how strong I was. I earned a spot on a SEAL team and gave my life over to them and was told I was a team player and valuable as a SEAL. When I was injured, people still told me that I could use my computer skills to help others. It hurt that I couldn't be out in the field, but I did the best I could to help anyone and everyone I could. I enjoyed it. But I have to tell you, Mel, I've never been happier in my entire life than I've been lying next to you here in my bed. My ring on your finger, my come coating your insides, and hopefully my baby growing in your belly. I love you. I'll protect you and Akilah and any children we might have with my life. *You* are what I've waited my entire life for. *You* are why I lost my leg. *You* are my reason for being here. You make me happy just the way you are."

Melody knew there was nothing she could say that would sum up how happy she was, and how much she loved her husband. She settled for the completely understated statement of, "I love you too, Tex."

# Chapter Twenty-Nine

PENELOPE TURNER, THE so-called Army Princess, stood at attention in her dress uniform and watched as two coffins were lowered into the ground at Arlington National Cemetery. Lieutenant James D. Love and Sergeant Richard S. Hess were being laid to rest in a private ceremony. She watched as two men she never had a chance to get to know were buried and thanked for their service to their country.

Deep down, Penelope couldn't shake the survivor's guilt she continued to feel.

She'd met with therapists and had some long talks with her brother, but she still couldn't get rid of the feeling that if it wasn't for her, these two brave men would still be alive today, laughing and joking with their friends and family. She vowed to find some sort of therapy group back home in San Antonio. She wanted to find others who might have gone through something similar to what she did…she probably wouldn't be able to find anyone who'd been kidnapped by a terrorist group and held for four months, but there had to be others out there who'd been held against their will and had some of the bad feelings churning inside them as she did.

Penelope looked over at the family members who'd gathered to pay their respects. She only knew what she'd read in the newspapers, but she assumed the gathering included their parents, grandparents, sisters, brothers, sisters-in-law, brothers-in-law, and even an aunt and uncle or two. Neither man was married, not that it made Penelope feel any better.

She watched as the family members left and the cemetery workers continued their work to bury the coffins in the ground. She stood and watched as the dirt was tamped down. She stood still even as a light rain began to fall.

Cade, as well as all the other firefighters had offered to come with her today, but she'd declined. It meant the world to her that Moose, Crash, Squirrel, Chief, Taco, and Driftwood had even offered. They weren't the touchy-feely kind of men, and knowing they cared enough about her as a member of their team was enough to make her break into tears.

Penelope sighed once, continuing to mourn the life of Lieutenant Love, who'd copiloted the plane that had gotten her out of the shithole that was the refugee camp and her temporary prison. She thought about Sergeant Hess. She'd never spoken to him, but he'd been the one to grasp her hand and help her onboard the MH-60. She'd looked into his eyes and seen nothing but confidence that they'd get the hell out of there in one piece.

She turned to leave—and stopped abruptly.

Standing behind her in a single-file line, at attention, were seven men, all in their Navy dress white uniforms. They wore no medals, no ribbons, only their name badges. They stood there, supporting her, and supporting the two dead Army soldiers behind her.

Refusing to cry, Penelope walked slowly over to the men standing so stoically and still. Knowing she was probably making a fool out of herself, she started with the first man. His name tag read, "Keegan." She'd never met him, but supposed this was probably the elusive, Tex. Before she could chicken out, she stepped up to him and wrapped her arms around him, hugging him tightly for a moment, before letting go and stepping back. "Thank you for finding us, Tex," she said softly, watching as the man nodded in return, but didn't say anything.

She moved to the next man in line. His nametag said, "Cooper," but she knew him as Dude, the man who'd first freed her from her prison. He was ready for her, and hugged her back when she wrapped her arms around him. "Thank you," Penelope said softly.

Then it was Benny's turn. His nametag read "Sawyer." She hugged him, and again, simply said, "Thank you."

Penelope moved down the line of men, hugging each one in turn. "Reed", otherwise known to her as Mozart; "Knox" who was Cookie; and "Powers" who was Abe. To him, she said "Thank you," but added, "You looked like shit the last time I saw you, glad to see you clean up well."

Ignoring his chuckle, Penelope moved to the last man in line. Wolf. The man in charge. The man who'd taken responsibility of this group and had moved heaven and earth to get her the hell out of Turkey and away from ISIS. The man she knew she'd never forget as long as she lived.

She wrapped her arms around him and felt him hug her back so hard, he lifted her off the ground in his embrace. "Thank you, Wolf. Thank you for not giving up on me." She wasn't expecting his response.

He eased her back to the ground, but didn't let go of her. "Thank *you*, Tiger, for being the kind of woman, and soldier, who could hold on until we could get there. Go live your life in peace. You've earned every second of happiness you can get. You've got seven big brothers in us now. We'll be watching out for you. Wherever you go, whatever you do, if you need us, all you have to do is ask."

Penelope felt Wolf move his hands down her back and rest on her ass for a moment before he let her go. It surprised her, but she figured it was an accident. The seven men saluted her, then left, fading back into the trees. She watched as they disappeared, not bothering to wipe away the tears that fell from her eyes and dripped down her face.

She turned to walk back to her car. She was spending the night in Washington DC, the President was awarding her with the Bronze Star the next day in a very public and televised event. She wasn't very excited about it, knowing there were others way braver than she'd been who would never be recognized publically and couldn't even tell anyone they'd been over there with her. But she'd take the reward on behalf of Lieutenant Love and Sergeants Hess, Black, White, and Wilson, and even that poor Australian soldier who had been killed in front of her eyes. Penelope thought about the Delta Force soldiers as well, they'd never get any recognition, other than her undying thanks and devotion.

The war with ISIS wasn't going to end anytime soon, but Penelope was done fighting it. She'd met with her commander and they'd agreed she was done with the military. She had a few more commitments she had to the government, but for all intents and purposes, she was free to be a full-time firefighter for the rest of her life. Her honorable discharge papers would be waiting for her when she got home.

She put her hands in her back pockets as she wandered down the too-long row of tombstones. Feeling something strange, she pulled her hand out and stared down at the small black object in her hand.

What the hell?

She unwrapped the folded piece of paper and found a small pendent in the shape of a Maltese Cross. The paper it had been wrapped in said, *Our men rescued us, and since they rescued you too, you're now one of us. Wear this and you'll never be lost again.*

Penelope thought about it and finally smiled for the first time that day. It sounded like it was a gift from the wives of the SEALs who had rescued her. Not only that, but apparently it was also a tracker like the men, and their women, wore. Wolf had slipped it into her pocket.

A tracker.

His words suddenly made sense and her smile grew. They'd be watching over her. It felt good. Right. She felt better for the first time in a long time. If she ever needed anyone at her back again, she not only had her firefighting buddies, but she had an entire SEAL team, and apparently their wives, as well.

Feeling stronger than she had in a long time, Sergeant Penelope Turner took a deep breath and straightened her shoulders. She'd make it through today. Then tomorrow. Then the next day. Then the next day after that. No problem. Piece of cake.

**The End**

# Author's Note

This is the end of the SEAL of Protection Series, but as you can probably imagine it's not the end of the road for some of your most loved characters. The Delta Force team you were introduced to in this story gets their own series. Of course you'll see Penelope and her firefighting teammates in a future series as well. And if you couldn't tell, Tex will continue to be the behind-the-scenes lifesaver in future books. That man knows everyone!

Thank you for your love and interest in my SEAL team. I never dreamed you'd fall as much in love with them as I did as I was writing them. In the meantime, check out the Badge of Honor series, featuring law enforcement heroes, and of course, Tex makes an appearance as well.

# Discover other titles by Susan Stoker

**Delta Force Heroes Series**

*Rescuing Rayne*
*Assisting Aimee (loosely related to DF)*
*Rescuing Emily*
*Rescuing Harley*
*Rescuing Kassie (TBA)*
*Rescuing Casey (TBA)*
*Rescuing Wendy (TBA)*
*Rescuing Mary (TBA)*

**Badge of Honor: Texas Heroes Series**

*Justice for Mackenzie*
*Justice for Mickie*
*Justice for Corrie*
*Justice for Laine (novella)*
*Shelter for Elizabeth*
*Justice for Boone*
*Shelter for Adeline (TBA)*
*Justice for Sidney (TBA)*
*Shelter for Blythe (TBA)*
*Justice for Milena (TBA)*
*Shelter for Sophie (TBA)*
*Justice for Kinley (TBA)*
*Shelter for Promise (TBA)*
*Shelter for Koren (TBA)*
*Shelter for Penelope (TBA)*

**SEAL of Protection Series**

*Protecting Caroline*

*Protecting Alabama*

*Protecting Fiona*

*Marrying Caroline (novella)*

*Protecting Summer*

*Protecting Cheyenne*

*Protecting Jessyka*

*Protecting Julie (novella)*

*Protecting Melody*

*Protecting the Future*

**Beyond Reality Series**

*Outback Hearts*

*Flaming Hearts*

*Frozen Hearts*

**Writing as Annie George**

*Stepbrother Virgin (erotic novella)*

## Connect with Susan Online

***Susan's Facebook Profile and Page:***

www.facebook.com/authorsstoker

www.facebook.com/authorsusanstoker

***Follow Susan on Twitter:***

www.twitter.com/Susan_Stoker

***Find Susan's Books on Goodreads:***

www.goodreads.com/SusanStoker

***Email:*** Susan@StokerAces.com

***Website:*** www.StokerAces.com

***To sign up for Susan's Newsletter go to:***

http://bit.ly/SusanStokerNewsletter

***Or text:*** STOKER to 24587 for text alerts on your mobile device

# About the Author

*New York Times*, *USA Today*, and *Wall Street Journal* Bestselling Author Susan Stoker has a heart as big as the state of Texas, where she lives, but this all-American girl has also spent the last fourteen years living in Missouri, California, Colorado, and Indiana. She's married to a retired Army man who now gets to follow *her* around the country.

She debuted her first series in 2014 and quickly followed that up with the SEAL of Protection Series, which solidified her love of writing and creating stories readers can get lost in.

If you enjoyed this book, or any book, please consider leaving a review. It's appreciated by authors more than you'll know.